ENCYCLOPEDIA BROWN TAKES THE CAKE!

**Other APPLE PAPERBACKS
you will want to read:**

Angie's First Case
by Donald J. Sobol
The Chicken Bone Wish
by Barbara Girion
Go Jump in the Pool!
by Gordon Korman
Kept in the Dark
by Nina Bawden
The TV Kid
by Betsy Byars
With a Wave of the Wand
by Mark Jonathan Harris

ENCYCLOPEDIA BROWN TAKES THE CAKE!

by
Donald J. Sobol
with
Glenn Andrews

Illustrations by
Ib Ohlsson

AN
APPLE
PAPERBACK

SCHOLASTIC INC.
New York Toronto London Auckland Sydney

For Dorothy Markinko
and Julie Fallowfield

ISBN 0-590-42901-9

12 11 10 9 8 7 6 5 4 3 2   0 1 2 3 4/9

Printed in the U.S.A.   11

CONTENTS

CHAPTER 1

THE CASE OF THE MISSING GARLIC BREAD

IDAVILLE looked like any other seashore town its size — on the outside. Inside, it was like no other place in America. For more than a year, no one had gotten away with breaking the law there.

Idaville's chief of police was Mr. Brown. He had a secret. Whenever he or his officers came up against a case too difficult for them, he knew what to do. He went home and talked to his only child, ten-year-old Leroy.

Over dinner, Leroy solved the case for him.

Leroy never spoke a word about the help he gave his father. He didn't want to appear different from other fifth-graders. But there was nothing he could do about his nickname, Encyclopedia.

An encyclopedia is a book or set of books filled with facts from A to Z, just like Encyclopedia's head.

He had read more books than almost anyone, and he never forgot what he read. He was like a bookmobile that runs on peanut butter and jelly sandwiches.

From fall to spring, Encyclopedia helped his father capture crooks. When school let out for the summer, he helped the children of the neighborhood, as well.

1

Every morning he hung his sign outside the garage.

BROWN DETECTIVE AGENCY
13 ROVER AVENUE
LEROY BROWN, PRESIDENT
No Case Too Small
25¢ Per Day Plus Expenses

One morning in late June, Encyclopedia and Sally Kimball, his partner, were seated in the garage when Josh Whipplewhite entered. Josh wore a mad and hungry look.

"You missed breakfast?" asked Encyclopedia.

"No," grumbled Josh. "Lunch."

"It's only ten o'clock in the morning!" exclaimed Sally. "You must have just flown in from France!"

"Naw, I never left Idaville," Josh replied. "But part of my lunch took off."

He explained. His mother had been fixing the food for his birthday party which was to start at one o'clock. She had made a big loaf of garlic bread and a chocolate cake. She had put them on the windowsill for a minute to get them out of the way.

"The cake and the garlic bread disappeared as if they'd flown — *pffft*!" Josh said. "My party's ruined!"

"You can have a party without garlic bread," Encyclopedia pointed out.

"But not without a birthday cake," declared Sally.

"Uh-uh," corrected Josh. "It's the garlic bread I'll miss. I'd rather have it than cake anytime."

He put a quarter on the gasoline can beside Encyclopedia. "I want to hire you," he said. "Find the thief!"

"Did you see anyone around your house at the time?" asked Encyclopedia.

"Three or four big boys," said Josh. "I didn't pay much attention. But one of them was called Bugs."

"Bugs — Bugs Meany!" cried Sally. "I knew it."

Bugs was the leader of a gang of tough older boys. They called themselves the Tigers. They should have called themselves the Pretzel Makers. They always tried to make dough the crooked way. The only things they hated more than honesty were soap and water.

Encyclopedia had dealt with Bugs in the past. Almost every week he had to stop the Tigers from cheating the children of the neighborhood.

"I'm pretty sure the Tigers made off with your garlic bread and birthday cake," he said. "Come with us."

The Tigers' clubhouse was an unused toolshed behind Mr. Sweeney's auto body shop. Bugs Meany, Duke Kelly, Spike Larsen, and Rocky Graham were inside, sitting on orange crates and chewing parsley.

Bugs chewed a little faster when he saw Encyclopedia, Sally, and Josh approaching.

"What's this?" he called. "Winter must have come early this year. The nuts are falling out of the trees."

Encyclopedia was used to Bugs's greetings. He ignored the remark.

"This is Josh Whipplewhite," he said. "Earlier this morning you four stole a birthday cake and a loaf of garlic bread from his kitchen windowsill."

"Stole?" exclaimed Bugs. He smote his forehead as if he couldn't believe anyone would accuse him of stealing. "We've been right here in the clubhouse all morning eating rabbit food. Got to get our vitamins."

"You unwashed ape," said Sally. "You're lying."

Bugs tilted his nose. "What makes you so sure, Miss Smarty?"

"Your lips are moving," snapped Sally.

Bugs grew red. "You prove I'm not honest in word and deed, and us Tigers will buy this little whipple-dipple kid another cake and a loaf of garlic bread."

"Agreed," said Encyclopedia quickly. He moved off to the side and powwowed with Sally and Josh.

"All we have to do is sniff their breath," whispered Josh. "Garlic leaves a terrible smell."

"They thought of that," Sally said. "They're chewing parsley on purpose. Parsley will sweeten even a camel's breath."

"Well, somebody ought to take a whiff just the same," Josh said. "But not me. It's my tenth birthday, and I want to live to be eleven."

Sally looked at Encyclopedia. The boy detective looked away. He had no desire to have his nose bitten by an angry Tiger.

"Boys," Sally said disgustedly. "All right, *I'll* do it."

She marched up to Bugs. "Open your mouth if you dare, you runaway from a bathtub."

Bugs seemed to be waiting for the command. He opened his mouth willingly.

Sally put her nose close. She did the same with Duke, Spike, and Rocky. They breathed heavily into her face and grinned.

She returned to Encyclopedia and Josh, defeated.

"The parsley got rid of the evidence, darn it," she said. "Bugs's breath is better than usual."

"There goes my lunch party," groaned Josh.

"Not yet," said Encyclopedia. "I think I can prove the Tigers stole the garlic bread and birthday cake."

HOW?

(Turn to page 114 for the solution to
The Case of the Missing Garlic Bread.)

CHAPTER 2

KITCHEN
BASICS

JOSH Whipplewhite took Encyclopedia and Sally home with him. Excitedly he told his mother how the detectives had bested the Tigers.

Mrs. Whipplewhite looked amazed. She looked more amazed after counting the money that the Tigers had given Josh.

"There is just enough to buy ingredients for more garlic bread and another birthday cake," she said.

She turned to America's Sherlock Holmes in sneakers. "You must be as good as Josh has been telling me," she said. "But I don't understand about the Tigers. Why did they pay for what they stole? They're big and strong. They could have chased you away."

"They know better," Josh said, beaming. "Bugs Meany has tried his bullying act several times. Sally squashed him flatter than a prune Danish every time they fought."

Josh wasn't fibbing. Sally was the best athlete in the fifth grade. And she was the only one, boy or girl, under twelve who could punch out Bugs Meany. Whenever they had tangled, Bugs had ended on the ground mumbling,

"Deal the cards," or some other line from dreamland.

"You two are quite a team," Mrs. Whipplewhite said to the detectives. She brought out milk and oatmeal cookies and placed them on the kitchen table. "Perhaps you'd like to help make Josh another birthday cake and garlic bread. You could —"

"Mom," Josh broke in. "They're detectives. They have a business to run."

"Oh, but we'd like to help," said Encyclopedia, who was always eager to learn. "Besides, business will be slow for a few days. Whenever Bugs is caught at some mischief, he lies low for a spell."

"And with the Fourth of July approaching, a lot of kids have left the neighborhood," Sally put in. "We could go without a customer for days."

"Then perhaps you'd like to help make the food for the party?" Mrs. Whipplewhite asked.

"That'd be neat!" exclaimed Encyclopedia.

Mrs. Whipplewhite got out a red crayon and a sheet of paper. "If we're going to do a lot of cooking, we'd better have some rules," she advised. She made up a sign and tacked it onto the kitchen bulletin board. It read:

1. Always wear oven mitts when you are putting things into and taking them out of the oven. Ask for help if you need it.

2. Handles on all pots have to be turned toward the back of the stove so nothing will be knocked over.

3. Plan ahead. Read the recipe all the way through before you start. Get things ready.

4. *The main rule*: Clean up as you go.

Mrs. Whipplewhite taught all the children how to use knives and a swivel-bladed vegetable peeler. Here's what she told them:

• Always work away from yourself and make sure your fingers aren't where they might be cut.

• Use sharp knives. (They're much safer than dull ones.)

• Always use a cutting board. (Never cut on the counter!)

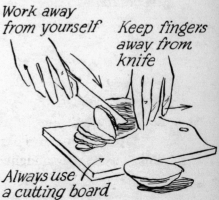

Work away from yourself

Keep fingers away from knife

Always use a cutting board

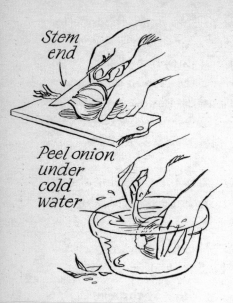

Stem end

Peel onion under cold water

To peel onions:

Cut off the stem end. Now, working under cold water, pull off the skin. (This method keeps you from crying when you work with onions.)

To peel potatoes, carrots, cucumbers, etc.:

Hold the vegetable near its top while you use a swivel-bladed vegetable peeler in your other hand to peel the bottom half of the vegetable, working away from you. Now turn the vegetable around and peel the other half. Be extra careful that your fingers aren't down so far that they'll be peeled instead of the vegetable. In the case of carrots and cucumbers, cut a thin slice off each end before beginning to peel.

Swiwel-blade vegetable knife

Blade moves as it peels vegetables.

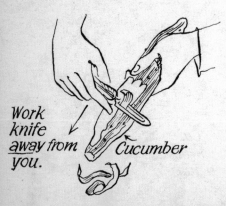

Work knife away from you.

Cucumber

To mince, dice, or chop onions:

Start with peeled, halved onions, placed cut side down on

a cutting board. Cutting from the stem end up toward the root, make a number of cuts up to, but not through, the root end. For minced onions, which are the smallest pieces, make many cuts, close to each other. The wider the space between cuts, the bigger the pieces will be. (Diced onions are in bigger pieces than minced; chopped are bigger still.) Now cut across the onion, just as though you were slicing it. Once more, the closer your cuts are to each other, the smaller the pieces will be. When you're finished, you will have a little piece of root end left, which you don't use.

First place the onion flat-side down and make cuts up to, but not through, the root end. Root end

Then cut straight across

To slice vegetables:

For onions and potatoes, the main thing is to have them lie flat while you work on them, which means they should be cut in half. Cut onions from the stem end right through the root end. Cut po-

Cut onion right through root end.

Then place onion flat-side down and cut across

Root end

Cut potatoes lengthwise

Hold several carrots together and slice straight across.

tatoes lengthwise. Place the vegetable halves flat side down on the cutting board. Slice whatever size pieces you want by cutting across. To slice carrots, hold several of them together, pressing them down on the cutting board, and then cut across.

To preheat ovens:

To preheat means to turn the oven on, set at the temperature given, and allow at least 20 minutes for it to reach the proper temperature. In some ovens, a light will go out to show you when the temperature is right.

To grease pans for baking:

To grease a baking pan or cookie sheet, put about one tablespoon of butter or margarine on a piece of waxed paper or a paper towel and rub the butter or margarine all over the bottom and sides of the pan until they are well coated.

CHAPTER 3

THE CASE OF
THE FOURTH OF JULY
ARTIST

ALTHOUGH Chester Jenkins could outeat a hippopotamus, he was always neat and clean. His mouth had been his target for so long that he never missed.

When he came into the Brown Detective Agency, however, his mouth was filled with words only.

"The Fourth of July is tomorrow," he said. "We ought to celebrate."

"I know your idea of celebrating," Sally said. "Food, food, and more food. Okay, let's have a party."

"With lots to eat?" Chester asked eagerly.

"With all the food you can stuff down," Encyclopedia assured him, "and enough left over for the rest of us."

The detectives called all their friends who hadn't gone out of town for the summer. Everyone thought the party was a great idea.

The children chipped in and bought the ingredients they would need. Mrs. Brown allowed them to store everything in her kitchen. She promised to let them use her best recipes and to help with any problems.

The next morning almost every child in Idaville and

most of the grown-ups went downtown to watch the big Fourth of July parade. There were three brass bands, a bagpipe band, a drum and bugle corps, and floats of all kinds.

Encyclopedia and Sally stood on the curb and applauded. They were cheering the new Miss Idaville, who was going by on a float with the mayor, when Chester rushed up.

"Come quick!" he blurted. "It's the chance of a lifetime!"

"Did a hamburger truck overturn?" Sally inquired.

"No, Wilford Wiggins passed the word," Chester answered. "He's holding a secret meeting behind Turner's Drugstore in ten minutes — just for kids. No grown-ups allowed!"

Encyclopedia crinkled his nose. Wilford Wiggins was a high school dropout and as hardworking as a flat tire. He spent his time dreaming up ways to get rich quick by cheating the children of the neighborhood.

"Wilford would try to sell electric forks to people on a hunger strike," Encyclopedia said.

"Today is different," Chester insisted. "I tell you, it's the chance of a lifetime!"

"The chance of Wilford's lifetime, you mean," Sally said. "He's never had so many kids to cheat. What's he selling?"

"He's going to raffle off a picture of the Liberty Bell that was painted on July 4, 1776," Chester replied. "The painting must be worth a fortune, but for us little kids, the tickets are only two dollars each."

"Two dollars? I think we'd better go to Wilford's art show," Encyclopedia said grimly.

When the detectives and Chester reached the alley behind Turner's Drugstore, dozens of children were already there. Wilford stood on a stepladder. He clutched a framed painting of the Liberty Bell.

"Here it is, my friends," he called out. "For only two dollars you can have a chance to win this magnificent, historical work of art."

He raised the painting above his head so that everyone could see it.

"My ancestor, Nathaniel Tarbox Wiggins, painted it on the very day our country was born," Wilford bellowed. "See, there's the date, right below the artist's signature in the corner."

Encyclopedia was standing too far back to see the details. But knowing Wilford, he had no doubt that the date, July 4, 1776, and the signature, Nathaniel Tarbox Wiggins, were on the painting.

Suddenly, Bugs Meany pushed and elbowed his way to the front.

"I was in Philadelphia last year and saw the Liberty Bell in person," Bugs said. "It has a crack in it. So quit playing your tonsils. That picture is a fake!"

"Now what have we here?" exclaimed Wilford. "A student of history? Step forward, friend, and take a closer look."

Bugs sneered and moved nearer the painting. He stared. His face reddened.

"I see the crack," he admitted sheepishly.

He dug into his pocket for two dollars with which to buy a raffle ticket. Several children started forming a line behind him.

The others in the crowd chattered excitedly. A picture that old had to be worth more than two dollars. It might even be worth hundreds — no, *thousands* — of dollars!

Sally looked concerned. "I just hate to see Wilford rake in two dollars from every kid here," she said to Encyclopedia. "Could the painting be the real thing?"

Encyclopedia didn't answer. It was time to act.

"Hold on, Wilford," he shouted. "When did this ancestor of yours die?"

Wilford hesitated. He hadn't noticed the detective in the crowd. He took a moment to put on a confident air.

"If you must know, Nathaniel Tarbox Wiggins lived to the ripe old age of eighty-seven. You can look it up," he said. "He didn't die until the year — let me see — 1822. So what?"

"So he didn't paint that picture on July 4, 1776, retorted Encyclopedia. "What's more, he didn't paint it at all."

WHY WAS ENCYCLOPEDIA SO CERTAIN?

(Turn to page 115 for the solution to
The Case of the Fourth of July Artist.)

CHAPTER 4

THE FOURTH OF JULY PARTY

CHESTER Jenkins was impatient. "Let's get started cooking the food for our party," he urged.

"Golly," Sally said. "I almost forgot."

"I never forgot for a minute!" Chester said.

Chester took his appetite straight to the Brown kitchen. Encyclopedia, Sally, and the friends they had invited for the Fourth of July party had trouble keeping up with him.

Mrs. Brown settled Chester down. She assured him that she would help with the cooking. All the food would turn out just right.

With that, Chester became her number one assistant. He followed instructions faithfully and never stole a taste ahead of time.

For Encyclopedia, working in his kitchen had meant lending a hand with the dishes. He had never tried making anything harder than a sandwich, usually peanut butter and jelly. Real cooking, he was discovering, was fun.

Here's what he and his friends had:

Oven-Fried Chicken
Tomato Salad with Snappy Dressing
Potato Salad
Pickled Beets

Red, White, and Blue Shortcake

All recipes serve 6.

OVEN-FRIED CHICKEN

2 chickens, each weighing about 2½ pounds, cut up

8 tablespoons butter or margarine, at room temperature

½ cup flour

1 teaspoon seasoned salt

1 teaspoon regular salt

1 teaspoon paprika

You will need:

paper towels

paper bag

baking pan(s)

1. Preheat oven to 350°F.

2. Dry chicken pieces thoroughly with a paper towel. Pull off any big pieces of fat. Rub the butter or margarine all over the chicken pieces.

3. Mix the flour, both salts, and paprika in a paper bag. Shake the chicken in this, two or three pieces at a time, until thoroughly coated. Put the pieces, skin side up, on a big, lightly greased baking pan. The pieces shouldn't touch each other. (Use two baking pans if you have to.)

4. Bake at 350°F for 25 minutes, then turn heat up to 400°F and bake 15 minutes more, or until chicken is nice and brown.

TOMATO SALAD WITH SNAPPY DRESSING

Lettuce leaves
4 big, beautiful, ripe tomatoes, at room temperature
Snappy Salad Dressing (see below)

You will need:
large platter or individual salad plates
small bowl

1. Wash lettuce leaves in cold water. Dry. Tear into bite-sized pieces. Use to line a large platter or 6 salad plates.

2. Slice tomatoes into rings about ¼ inch thick. Arrange them on top of lettuce. (Don't use the slices from the top and bottom of each tomato.)

3. Make Snappy Salad Dressing:

1 tablespoon vinegar
¼ teaspoon salt
½ teaspoon prepared mustard
½ teaspoon light brown sugar
3 tablespoons salad oil

Mix the vinegar, salt, mustard, and light brown sugar together in a small bowl, then stir in the salad oil.

4. Spoon the dressing slowly onto the tomatoes.

If Chester — or anyone else with a really big appetite — is coming to your party, you'd better use six tomatoes instead of four. The salad dressing will be enough for either amount.

POTATO SALAD
---

  6 medium-sized boiled potatoes
  4 hard-boiled eggs
  ½ cup mayonnaise
  ¼ cup minced onion (or 2 tablespoons
     instant onion mixed with 2 tablespoons water)
  2 stalks celery, thinly sliced
  ½ cup sweet pickle relish
  2 tablespoons cider vinegar
  1½ teaspoons salt
  Lettuce leaves, washed in cold water, then dried

You will need:
  large pot
  egg slicer (optional)
  slotted spoon
  large bowl
  salad bowl or platter

1. Peel potatoes and cut them into little squares. (If you don't have boiled potatoes on hand, wash your raw ones and cook them in a pot of water with a teaspoon of salt for about 25 minutes, or until you can stick a fork all the way through them. Remove from water very carefully — it's a good idea to have a grown-up help with this — and let them cool.)

2. Peel eggs. Cut them in little pieces. If you have an egg slicer, you can put them through it, first one way, then the other. (No cooked eggs in the refrigerator? Then put

eggs in a pot with enough cold water to cover them. Add a tablespoon of vinegar. Bring water to a boil, then turn down heat and cook slowly for ten minutes. Move eggs carefully with a slotted spoon to a bowl full of cold water.)

3. Mix all the other ingredients except the lettuce together in a mixing bowl. Stir in the potato and egg pieces. Keep in refrigerator until you're ready to eat.

4. To serve, line a salad bowl or platter with the lettuce leaves. Top with the potato salad.

PICKLED BEETS

    2 1-pound cans sliced beets
    ¼ cup honey
    ⅓ cup cider vinegar

You will need:
    saucepan
    bowl

1. Open the cans. Drain the juice into a saucepan. Put the beets into a bowl.

2. Add the honey and vinegar to the beet juice in the saucepan. Bring the mixture just to a boil, then turn the heat down and simmer for 10 minutes.

3. Pour the beet juice liquid over the beets in their bowl. When the liquid is cool, cover the bowl and put it in the refrigerator to chill for at least 2 hours.

RED, WHITE, AND BLUE SHORTCAKE

1. First, make the biscuits (you can do this an hour or two ahead).

     2 cups unsifted flour
     1 tablespoon double-acting baking powder
     ⅛ teaspoon salt
     1 tablespoon sugar
     1 cup (1 8-ounce carton) heavy cream

You will need:
     mixing bowl
     rolling pin
     3-inch round cookie cutter
     baking sheet

Preheat oven to 450°F. Mix the dry ingredients in a bowl. Now, using a fork, gently stir in the heavy cream. Mix only until the dry ingredients are moistened. Turn the dough out onto a floured surface. Flour your hands, too. Then pat the dough together until it is smooth. Using a floured rolling pin, gently roll the dough out ½ inch thick. Cut out six big biscuits with a floured 3″ cutter. You may have to re-roll the dough.

Place on an ungreased baking sheet. Bake for 10–15 minutes or until the biscuits have risen and are light brown.

When they have cooled enough to handle, cut them in half through the middle so that each half is a big circle. Put them back together, and just let them sit until you need them.

2. Get the red, white, and blue topping ready (start this when you put the biscuits in the oven).

   1 pint strawberries, or 1 12-ounce box frozen
      sliced strawberries
   1 pint whole blueberries, fresh or frozen
   6 to 8 tablespoons sugar (see below)
   1 cup heavy cream or 1 can instant whipped-
      cream topping

If you use fresh strawberries, wash them, remove the green part, and cut them into thin slices. Put them in a bowl with 3 tablespoons of sugar and stir. Put blueberries in another bowl with 3 tablespoons of sugar. Mash them a little with a fork. If you use cream, beat it with 2 table-spoons of sugar with an electric mixer, an egg beater, or a whisk until it's light and fluffy. Put everything in the refrigerator.

3. When you're ready to serve, put one biscuit on each plate. Put some strawberries and blueberries on the bottom half of each biscuit, then put the biscuit tops back on. Now put on the red, white, and blue topping: a stripe of strawberries on the left, a stripe of blueberries on the right, and whipped cream down the middle.

CHAPTER 5

THE CASE OF
THE OVEN MITT

ON the day Bella Feinfinger began working part-time in her father's kitchenware shop, Encyclopedia and Sally dropped by to wish her well.

Bella was alone in the store except for one customer, Hermes Jones. He was examining oven mitts, which Bella had piled upon the counter.

"I'm looking for a wedding anniversary gift for my mom," Hermes told the detectives. "I bought my dad bookends yesterday. Do you think my mom would like one of these oven mitts?"

"I'm sure she would," Sally said. "They're all lovely."

"So are the spoon rests and the toaster covers," Hermes said. "I can't decide."

Bella rolled her eyes at the detectives. Obviously, Hermes had been trying to make up his mind for some time.

The detectives didn't want to confuse Hermes any further by offering suggestions. So they simply wished Bella good luck with her job and headed for the door.

"I'll see you at my birthday party Saturday?" Hermes called.

"We'll be there," Encyclopedia said. He was glad that kids don't have to decide when to have birthdays. Otherwise, Hermes would still be three years old.

Saturday arrived on time, but the detectives were late reaching Hermes's house. Most of the other guests — Nancy Frumm, Pablo Pizarro, Chips Davis, Charlie Stewart, and Magnolia Peabody — were already in the living room. Only Bella Feinfinger was missing.

"Gee, thanks," Hermes said as the detectives handed him their presents. He laid them at his place on the dining room table.

"C'mon and join the gang," he said, leading the detectives into the living room.

Encyclopedia recalled Hermes's problems at the kitchenware store.

"Did you get your mother's gift?" he asked.

"Yep, and it's beautiful," Hermes replied.

"What is it?" inquired Magnolia, who was inclined to be nosy.

"It's a secret," Hermes replied.

"Aw, tell us," Pablo urged.

"Yes, what did you get her?" Nancy pleaded.

"You're among friends," Chips said. "Tell us."

"We'll keep your secret," Charlie assured him.

"An oven mitt," Hermes whispered, reluctantly but proudly. "It's on the top shelf in my closet if you want a peek. My folks' anniversary is Tuesday."

Chips and Pablo weren't interested in looking at an oven mitt. But Magnolia started up the stairs. She got Nancy to go with her.

Just then the doorbell rang.

It was Bella Feinfinger. Her eyes were red, as if from crying. In her fist she clutched a crumpled handkerchief.

She gave Hermes her gift and blurted, "I must speak with Encyclopedia and Sally."

Hermes nodded and led her and the detectives into the sun parlor. So they could not be overheard, he closed the glass doors.

"Sit down, Bella," Sally said gently. "Now, how can we help you?"

"Somebody robbed the store," she said. "It could only have happened on Wednesday, when I was minding it. Two expensive electric mixers were stolen."

The detectives questioned her quietly. There wasn't much, however, that she could tell them.

The mixers were taken from the storeroom in the rear of the store. Her father had told her always to keep the door leading from the storeroom to the back alley locked. But early that morning she had put out the garbage, and she had forgotten to lock the door on her way back.

"The mixers must have been taken Wednesday," she said. "After I waited on Hermes, I went into the storeroom and found the outside door ajar. My dad didn't discover that the mixers were gone until this morning."

"How can you be so sure that the mixers were taken while you were with Hermes?" Sally asked.

"Because that's the only time the back door was left unlocked," Bella said.

"Has your father punished you?" Encyclopedia asked.

"No," Bella said. "He just told me to be more careful in the future."

She broke into sobs. After a minute she wiped her eyes and blew her nose.

"I feel so guilty," she whimpered. "So stupid!"

"You can't be so hard on yourself," Sally said.

"I must find the thief and get back the two mixers," Bella exclaimed. "I must!"

"Strange," Encyclopedia murmured.

"What?" demanded Sally.

"Only two mixers were stolen."

"I don't understand . . ." Sally said.

"If the thief was a grown-up, he would have taken more," Encyclopedia explained. "He would have used a car or a truck to cart off a real load."

Bella looked at Encyclopedia with a ray of hope. "Then you think the thief is a kid?"

"Certainly," said Encyclopedia. "You can't carry much in your arms or on a bicycle. Two mixers are plenty."

"Do you know who it is?" Bella asked.

"Yes, and fortunately the thief is right under this roof — a guest at the party."

"For mercy sakes, Encyclopedia," Sally almost shouted. "Who is it?"

"Why, the thief is . . ."

WHO?

(Turn to page 116 for the solution to
The Case of the Oven Mitt.)

CHAPTER 6

HERMES'S BIRTHDAY BRUNCH

THERE was no point in spoiling Hermes's birthday party. So Encyclopedia took Nancy quietly aside. He told her how he knew that she had stolen the two mixers.

Nancy's face went blank. Suddenly tears filled her eyes. "Are you going to call the police?" she whispered fearfully.

"Will you return the two mixers?" asked Encyclopedia.

"Yes," she promised in a small voice.

"Then the case is closed," the detective said.

As if nothing had been said between them, Encyclopedia and Nancy joined in the party fun. It was after the second game of charades that Hermes made his announcement.

"We have something else to celebrate today besides my birthday," he said. "Charlie Stewart's tooth collection was started five years ago today."

Charlie blushed as everyone cheered. His tooth collection was the finest in Idaville. He kept it in a flowered cookie jar.

"We ought to do something special for Charlie's teeth," Encyclopedia suggested.

"We are," Hermes replied. "My birthday brunch will have food that looks like teeth!"

"Ugh," muttered Sally.

"Don't worry," Hermes said. "Some of the food looks like teeth. Some of it will just have a bite in it."

"Oh, is that ever corny!" Sally protested.

"Corn kernels look like teeth," pointed out Encyclopedia.

"Exactly," Hermes said. "We're going to start with corny chowder."

Here is the menu for the double celebration.

Corny Chowder

Toothburger Stew
Cole Slaw
Cucumber Mouthfuls

Tooth Collector's Chocolate Cake
with Tooth Collector's Frosting —
and Teeth

CORNY CHOWDER

3 cans (about 16 ounces each) cream-style corn
1 small can (about 8 ounces) white whole-
   kernel corn, drained
1½ quarts (6 cups) milk
3 tablespoons butter
½ teaspoon salt

You will need:
saucepan

Mix everything together in a saucepan. Cook over low heat, stirring often, just until it steams. Don't let it boil.

Makes 9 large servings. To serve a smaller group of 6, use only:

2 cans cream-style corn
1 small can white whole-kernel corn
4 cups milk
2 tablespoons butter
¼ teaspoon salt

TOOTHBURGER STEW

1½ pounds ground beef
⅓ cup minced onion (or 2½ tablespoons
   instant onion mixed with 2½ tablespoons water)
1½ 8-ounce cans tomato sauce
1 teaspoon salt
1½ cups macaroni, uncooked
3 cups water
1½ tablespoons grated cheese

You will need: large frying pan

1. Brown the ground beef in a large frying pan or saucepan
over medium heat, stirring and breaking it up with a fork
or wooden spoon as it cooks.

2. Add the onion, tomato sauce, salt, macaroni, and water.
Bring to a boil, then lower heat and cook very slowly,
uncovered, for 15 minutes, stirring occasionally. You might
have to add a little more water, *but* you want most of
the liquid to have disappeared by the time you're through.

3. Stir in the grated cheese.

Serves 9. To serve 6, use only:

1 pound ground beef
¼ cup onions (or 2 teaspoons instant onion)
1 can tomato sauce
1 teaspoon salt
1 cup macaroni
2 cups water
1 tablespoon grated cheese

COLE SLAW

1 package (about 1 pound) shredded cabbage
1 cup mayonnaise
2 tablespoons sugar
3 tablespoons vinegar
1 teaspoon mild prepared mustard
1 teaspoon celery seed (optional)

You will need:
   2 mixing bowls

Put the shredded cabbage in a bowl. Combine all the other ingredients, then mix with the cabbage. Keep in the refrigerator until you're ready to serve.

Serves 6 to 9.

CUCUMBER MOUTHFULS

You will need:
   vegetable peeler

Peel cucumbers with a vegetable peeler. Cut them in half lengthwise, then cut each section into 3 pieces (again cutting lengthwise). The seeds will make each section look like a big mouthful of teeth.

Use 3 cucumbers for 9 people or 2 cucumbers for 6.

TOOTH COLLECTOR'S
CHOCOLATE CAKE

1½ cups milk, lukewarm or at room temperature
1 tablespoon lemon juice
1 teaspoon pure vanilla
½ cup cocoa
2 cups sugar, in 2 parts (see below*)
1 stick (4 ounces) plus 2 tablespoons butter
   or margarine, at room temperature
2 eggs
2 cups plus 2 tablespoons pre-sifted flour
1 teaspoon baking soda
½ teaspoon salt

You will need:
   9-inch angel food cake pan
   electric mixer
   blender (optional)
   toothpick or cake tester
   cooling rack
   serving plate

1. Preheat oven to 350°F. Use the 2 tablespoons of butter
or margarine to grease a 9-inch angel food cake pan. Tip
the 2 tablespoons of flour around in the pan until it's
coated. Combine the milk and lemon juice in a 2-cup or
1-quart measuring cup. Let it sit until clabbered (slightly
thickened), then combine ½ cup of it with the vanilla,
cocoa, and 1 cup of the sugar*. Mix well. (An electric
blender does this job easily.) Set aside for now.

2. Beat the stick of butter until creamy, preferably using an electric mixer, then beat in the other cup of sugar,* adding about ¼ cup at a time. Beat in the eggs, one at a time.

3. Combine the rest of the flour with the baking soda and salt. Beating well each time, add ½ cup of the flour mixture to the butter mixture, then ⅓ of the remaining 1 cup of clabbered milk. Repeat until all of the flour mixture and milk are used, then beat in the cocoa mixture from above.

4. Pour the batter evenly into the prepared pan. Bake for 50 or 60 minutes, or until a toothpick or cake tester stuck into the middle of the cake comes out dry. If the cake's not ready, bake a little longer and test again.

5. Cool on a rack, still in the cake pan, for 30 minutes, or until the pan is cool enough to handle. Run a table knife around the edge where the cake meets the pan and also around the center tube. Now put a serving plate, bottom side up, over the cake pan. Holding on tight, turn the whole thing upside down, so the cake will fall onto the plate. When the cake is completely cool, frost with Tooth Collector's Frosting — and Teeth (see page 38).

This is a very dark cake, almost like a devil's food cake and will stay moist for several days if kept covered.

Serves 6 to 9.

TOOTH COLLECTOR'S FROSTING — AND TEETH

1 12-ounce package semisweet real chocolate bits
1 cup (1 8-ounce carton) sour cream
1 small roll prepared marzipan (you can buy
   7-ounce rolls of this in many supermarkets) or
2 ounces slivered blanched almonds

You will need:
double boiler

1. Melt the chocolate bits in a double boiler, stirring until they're all melted. Use very low heat. Remove from fire. Stir in the sour cream. Spread the frosting on the cake.

2. If you're using the marzipan, shape into little teeth and decorate the cake with them. If you can't find marzipan, slivered almonds make good teeth, too. Just stick them in all over the frosting.

Bicuspids look like this:

Bicuspid

Molars look like this:

Molar

CHAPTER 7

THE CASE OF
THE OVERSTUFFED
PIÑATA

ENCYCLOPEDIA was walking along Main Street one day
early in September when he sighted trouble.

Tim Gomez was standing halfway down the block
and looking madder than a flea on a stone dog. He was
holding a box and a piece of wrapping paper in one hand,
and he was glaring across the street at Bugs Meany.

Bugs was leaning against the wall of the post office
and balancing a toy bull in his hand. He was laughing
and joking with three of his Tigers—and watching Tim.

"Encyclopedia!" Tim cried. "Am I glad you came
along."

"What's going on?" the detective inquired.

"That no-good Bugs stole my bull!" exclaimed Tim.

He explained. His Aunt Maria, who lived on a farm
in the western part of the state, had sent him a papier-
mâché piñata shaped like a bull. Because there was post-
age due, he'd had to go to the post office to pick up the
package. As he opened it on the sidewalk, Bugs had come
by and grabbed the bull.

"Now Bugs says it's his," Tim grumped. "All I have
left is the box and the wrapping paper."

Encyclopedia tried to catch up. A piñata, he knew, was a decorated figure or jug. In Latin American countries piñatas filled with gifts are hung from the ceiling and broken on holidays. Children, wearing blindfolds, hit them with sticks until they break and the presents fall out.

The detective squinted across the street at the piñata bull Bugs was holding. Except for the horns, which were black, the bull was covered all over with little curls of tissue paper in strips of yellow, orange, and pink.

"I was in Hector's Department Store half an hour ago," the detective said. "I noticed a counter of piñatas— papier-mâché bulls and clay jars—because a lady accidentally knocked a jar and two bulls onto the hard floor. The jar broke, but the bulls just bounced."

"Did the bulls look like mine?" Tim asked anxiously.

"One of them did," replied Encyclopedia. "There were more like yours on the counter."

"Rats," Tim grunted. "Now Bugs can lie his head off. He'll swear that he bought my piñata bull at Hector's."

"And the salespeople will never remember whether he bought one or not," Encyclopedia added.

"Well, mine is different," Tim said. "My aunt always makes a little hole in the piñata and stuffs a lot of candy inside. She stuffs it so full it doesn't rattle."

"That's it!" Encyclopedia remarked. "Bugs won't know about the hole, and so you—"

"No good," Tim broke in. "My aunt seals the hole up so well that you can't see where it is from the outside. I'd have to break open the piñata to prove it."

"Bugs will never let you do that," commented Encyclopedia.

The detective closed his eyes and did some heavy thinking. He thought of how to trap Bugs into admitting he had stolen the bull from Tim.

Suddenly his eyes opened. "Let's have a talk with Bugs," he said, smiling.

As Encyclopedia and Tim started across the street, Bugs took a better grip on the bull.

"Get lost," he growled at the detective, "or I'll pound you so hard on the top of the head you'll have to reach up to pull on your sneakers."

Encyclopedia was quite used to Bugs's welcomes. Calmly he said, "Tim claims you stole that bull from him."

"Man, oh, man!" Bugs wailed. "I'm accused of everything! Listen, I haven't stolen a thing for weeks. I've gone straight."

"You couldn't go straight if you walked a tightrope!" yelped Tim.

Bugs made a fist, but then caught himself. "For your information, I just bought this bull at Hector's Department Store," he said.

"Come on, Bugs, wasn't it quite a while ago that you were at the store?" Encyclopedia said. "And haven't you done some other shopping since then?"

"I don't know what you're getting at," Bugs snapped. "I bought this bull just a few minutes ago. I was heading home when I saw this crazy kid coming out of the post office with nothing but that empty box and the piece of wrapping paper."

"I ought to wrap his head, the big liar!" Tim whispered to Encyclopedia.

"Sssh," Encyclopedia whispered back, watching Bugs's fist.

"I guess someone sent him a package with nothing in it," Bugs went on. "When he saw my bull, he pretended it belonged to him. Fat chance. Someone sent him an empty package to match his empty head."

"Are you sure you didn't do anything else after you bought the bull?" Encyclopedia asked.

"I told you once, didn't I?" Bugs's voice had risen shrilly. "What's the matter? Don't you believe the word of an honest boy?"

"Yes, I do," Encyclopedia said. "That's why I believe Tim."

WHAT MADE ENCYCLOPEDIA SO SURE?

(Turn to page 117 for the solution to
The Case of the Overstuffed Piñata.)

A MEXICAN
FIESTA

WHEN Tim called his Aunt Maria to thank her for sending him a piñata, he told her how Encyclopedia had saved his present by solving "The Case of the Overstuffed Piñata."

"I'd like to give your friend a reward," Tim's aunt said.

"Oh, Encyclopedia wouldn't take a reward," Tim answered. "I paid him his regular twenty-five-cent fee."

"I think he'll take this reward," his aunt said. "You just watch the mail for another box — a big one this time. And take it straight over to Encyclopedia's house before that Meany boy has a chance to snatch it."

A few days later, Tim came into the Browns' garage, walking backward and dragging a big box. Encyclopedia and Sally rushed to help him.

"I think this box is really for you, Encyclopedia," Tim said. "My aunt sent it when she heard what you'd done to save my piñata."

"Open it! Open it!" cried Sally.

The first thing inside the box was a note. "This is

an instant party kit," Encyclopedia read. "You can use it for a fiesta to celebrate Mexico's Independence Day."

"Mmm, that's September sixteenth," Sally said.

Encyclopedia nodded and read on. "You can have a tostada or taco party. There's everything here but the food, and I've sent you some easy recipes for that. Have the party outdoors or in a garage because it can get pretty messy."

The first thing to come out of the box was a brightly colored sheet. "Your aunt says to put two card tables together for a serving table and use this for a tablecloth," Encyclopedia said to Tim.

Next, out came six flags. They were green on the left, white in the middle, and red on the right. There was a seal on the white part.

"Mexico's flag," Encyclopedia said. "We can decorate the garage with them for the party."

Then came six big Mexican hats.

"We can do the Mexican hat dance!" Sally cried.

The rest of the box contained paper plates and paper napkins in bright colors; red, white, and green crepe paper for streamers; and a record with Mexican songs.

"Hooray!" Sally called out.

"Viva your Aunt Maria!" said Encyclopedia.

"Olé!" cried Tim.

Tostadas, Taco Shells, or Corn Chips
Refried Beans
Mexican Meat Mixture

Garnishes

Fruit Platter
Polvorones (Mexican Cookies)

All recipes serve 6, unless otherwise stated.

All the food for the main part of the meal is put out on a big table. First, a big plate or platter with the tostadas, taco shells, or corn chips. Next, a bowl or plate with the refried beans, then one with the meat mixture. Now put out all the garnishes, each one in its own little bowl or a small plate. Make sure each bowl or plate has its own spoon for serving.

You can either put the fruit platter and the cookies on the table from the beginning or bring them out later.

TOSTADAS, TACO SHELLS, OR CORN CHIPS

You will need:
    frying pan
    tongs
    paper towels

A tostada is a corn tortilla (pronounced *tore-TEE-yuh*), fried flat and crisp. You pile refried beans, a meat mixture, and whatever garnishes you want on it, and you hold it in your hands to eat it. It's a sort of edible plate.

A taco shell is a fried corn tortilla, too, but it has been folded in half. You fill it and eat it just as you do a tostada.

You will probably be able to buy tostadas or taco shells— fried and ready to use—in a supermarket, a Mexican market, or a Mexican restaurant. If not, many markets sell corn tortillas from which you can make your own tostadas. Just fry the tortillas one by one in a frying pan with about ¼ inch of oil until they are crisp, turning them carefully with tongs. Let them dry on paper towels. (Don't try to make taco shells at home, though. They're too tricky.)

If you can't find a place to buy tostadas, taco shells, or corn tortillas, you can still have a Mexican party. Just use corn chips (sometimes called tortilla chips). The only problem with them is that you have to put a plate under them and eat your meal with a fork.

REFRIED BEANS

You will need:
>   canned refried beans:
>   frying pan or saucepan
>   or
>   canned whole beans:
>   bowl
>   potato masher or fork
>   frying pan or saucepan

If you can buy canned refried beans, just put the contents of 2 16-ounce cans into a frying pan or saucepan with 3 tablespoons of salad oil or lard. Warm them up, stirring often, just before you're ready to serve.

If you can't find refried beans, use 2 16-ounce cans of pinto beans or red kidney beans and "refry" them as follows:

1. Drain off most of the liquid from the cans.

2. Put the beans into a bowl. Mash them with a potato masher or a fork. Don't worry if you don't get them absolutely smooth.

3. Put the mashed beans in a frying pan or saucepan with 3 tablespoons of salad oil. Warm them up, stirring often, just before you're ready to serve.

MEXICAN MEAT MIXTURE

1½ pounds ground beef
½ cup chopped onion (or 2 tablespoons
   instant onion mixed with ¼ cup water)
2 tablespoons salad oil or lard
1½ teaspoons chili powder
1 teaspoon salt
½ teaspoon ground cumin (optional)

You will need:
   frying pan or saucepan

1. Cook the ground beef and onion in the oil in a frying
pan or saucepan, stirring, just until all the meat changes
color from pink to light tan.

2. Add the chili powder, salt, and cumin (if you're using
it—it doesn't add hotness, but does make things taste
very Mexican). Cook and stir for 3 or 4 minutes more.

GARNISHES

Here are the garnishes to put out on your table:

1 cup lettuce, finely cut into shreds
2 tomatoes, chopped (cut them in half and
   scoop out the seeds first)
¾ cup grated cheese
1 cup (8 ounces) sour cream
1 bottle mild Mexican taco sauce or
   American chili sauce

You will need:
    separate bowl or plates and spoons
        for each garnish

Also, if you want, you can put out:

    Minced onions or scallions
    Sliced radishes
    Minced olives, either green or ripe (black)

Put each item in a separate bowl or on a little plate, and
give each one its own spoon.

FRUIT PLATTER

You will need:
    platter or bowl

Take a big platter or bowl and pile it full of all the fruits
you can find that can be eaten in your hand. Wash all
the fruit first. Polish the apples. Rub the fuzz off the
peaches under cold water. Arrange the fruit so it will look
pretty and you can see some of each kind. Drape clusters
of grapes over the top. If you have strawberries, scatter
them around the top. Here are some of the fruits you can
use:

Apples	Nectarines
Plums	Strawberries
Peaches	Figs
Bananas (in their skins)	Tangerines or tangelos
Navel oranges	Grapes
Apricots	Pears

You might want to try some unusual fruits, too, when they are in season. Some of these are kiwis, mangoes, small papayas, and persimmons. Pomegranates are fun, too—you eat only the seeds, which are delicious.

POLVORONES

(Mexican Cookies—pronounced *pole-vo-RONE-aze*)

>   ½ pound (2 sticks) butter, at room temperature
>   ½ cup unsifted confectioners' sugar
>   2 cups unsifted flour
>   ¼ teaspoon salt
>   1 teaspoon vanilla
>   ½ cup (or more) extra confectioners' sugar

You will need:
>   mixing bowls (2)
>   electric mixer (optional)
>   baking sheet
>   cooling rack

1. Put all the ingredients except the extra confectioners' sugar in a bowl, and mix them together thoroughly until they form a big ball. You can do this with a mixer or with your hands. (It's more fun with your hands.)

2. Cover the bowl with foil or plastic wrap. Chill in the refrigerator for at least an hour.

3. Preheat oven to 375°F.

4. Make the dough into 1-inch balls by rolling little pieces of it between the palms of your hands. Place the balls on an ungreased baking sheet. (They can be placed close together, but shouldn't touch each other.)

5. Bake for 15 minutes, or until the cookies are very light brown.

6. Put the extra confectioners' sugar in a small bowl. Roll the baked cookies in this one by one, then put them on a rack to cool. (The cookies should be rolled in the sugar soon after they come out of the oven, but they will be too hot to touch—so pick them up by holding a spoon in each hand, and use these to move the cookies and roll them in the confectioners' sugar.) If you want sweeter cookies, you can roll them in the confectioners' sugar one more time after they're cool.

Makes about 48 cookies.

CHAPTER 9

THE CASE OF
THE MISSING
WATCHGOOSE

ENCYCLOPEDIA was reading about the Roman Empire one Saturday morning in October when Candida Strong telephoned.

"Christopher Columbus Day is missing!" she wailed.

Encyclopedia stood firm. After all, Candida was so absentminded that she could lose her sense of direction in an elevator. For her, losing Christopher Columbus Day was really no worse than losing any other Monday.

"When did Christopher Columbus Day disappear?" the detective inquired. "Last year?"

"This morning—oh, you don't understand," Candida protested. "Christopher Columbus Day is a goose. You've got to find him!"

"I'm on my way," Encyclopedia said.

Candida lived at a plant nursery. She hurried out of the house as Encyclopedia alighted from the Number 9 bus.

"Thank goodness you're here," she said. "Christopher Columbus Day is the best watchgoose we have."

She explained. For several years her father had been

troubled by people stealing supplies from the nursery—
bales of peat moss, topsoil, even shrubs.

"At first Dad tried watchdogs," she said. "They had
to be chained, and so they were good only for the length
of the chain. Also, Dad was afraid they might hurt someone."

She waved toward a group of five geese.

"Those geese were the answer," she said. "They can't
fly. They just roam about the place, winter and summer.
All they want is a kiddie pool to splash around in and
a little corn. They do the job."

"If honking geese could save ancient Rome from the
Gauls sneaking in at night, they ought to protect a nursery," Encyclopedia agreed.

"Their beaks are like vises," Candida said. "I've seen
them drive off stray dogs that got into the henhouse."
She turned. "C'mon, I'll show you around."

The tour took fifteen minutes. Encyclopedia found
not a single clue to the missing goose. He did notice,
however, that the back of the nursery bordered on Den-
isen Park, the state camping grounds.

Monday—the day after tomorrow—was the real
Christopher Columbus Day. Families in station wagons
and mobile homes were arriving at the park for the long
holiday weekend.

"Let's look in the park," Encyclopedia suggested.
"Christopher Columbus Day may have gone exploring."

As they headed for the park, the detective asked if
Christopher Columbus Day knew his own name.

"Nope, geese are free spirits," Candida replied. "Besides, although we named the watchgeese after holidays, we call them all Flatfoot. It saves time."

Encyclopedia was both disappointed and relieved by the news. He wondered if he really could have walked through the park calling, "Here, Christopher Columbus Day!" Especially this weekend.

The two children split up, agreeing to meet by the entrance booth in three hours. Candida took the western half of the park to search, Encyclopedia the eastern.

For nearly two hours the detective asked campers if they had seen a runaway goose. No one had, though they were all interested and tried to be helpful. The only exception was a tall, muscular woman. She wore a dark brown shirt, cutoff jeans, and hiking shoes, and she carried a large red knapsack.

"A goose? Are you kidding me, sonny?" she grumbled, and never broke stride.

A few minutes later, Encyclopedia found three feathers by a bright new mobile home. He was examining them when a white-haired man came up to him.

"I'm chasing a goose," Encyclopedia explained. He held out the feathers.

The man examined them. "These are chicken feathers," he said. "I know. I used to have a farm in Iowa before I retired last year. Raised turkeys and Rhode Island Reds on the side."

Encyclopedia thanked the man and moved on. It was nearly noon.

Most of the campers whom he questioned during the next half-hour were eating lunch or preparing to eat. One woman remembered seeing several boys chasing a rooster earlier that morning. But no one had seen a goose.

Encyclopedia was getting hungry himself when he spied two men eating by a fire. As he approached, one of the men called out, "What's wrong, young fella? Hungry? Have some chicken. There's plenty."

The second man held a spit with several parts—wings, neck, breast, and thighs—stuck on it. He flicked his knife and sliced off some meat from the breast.

"Nothing like hot-off-the-fire chicken," he said with a chuckle. The knife, with a slice of dark meat dangling from the tip, he shoved at Encyclopedia.

"Much obliged," Encyclopedia mumbled, plucking the meat free. "Have you seen a goose around here?"

"No," the first man said. "Hey, wait . . . we passed a bunch of them on the way to the park. At a plant nursery. Some woman with a red knapsack was feeding them."

"I should have guessed!" Encyclopedia said, and hurried off.

He jogged the remainder of his search area without success. The woman with the red knapsack had vanished. Disappointed, he made his way back to the entrance to meet Candida.

She was waiting for him. "Any luck?"

"I have a lead," Encyclopedia said. "Did you see a big woman with a red knapsack?"

"And a dark brown shirt?" Candida asked. "Sure. She nearly walked over me. Was she in a rush!"

"She's a suspect . . ." His voice trailed off. Then he smacked his thigh and said, "How slow of me!"

"Oh, dear," Candida said. "For a moment I thought you knew where Christopher Columbus Day is."

"I do," replied the detective. "But I needed your help."

WHAT DID ENCYCLOPEDIA MEAN?

(Turn to page 118 for the solution to
The Case of the Missing Watchgoose.)

CHAPTER 10

AN ITALIAN
DINNER

CANDIDA was crushed. Her pet watchgoose was gone, never to honk again.

Encyclopedia and Sally did their best to cheer her up. They told jokes and tried to get her to play games. Encyclopedia nearly suggested Duck Duck Goose, but caught himself.

After an hour, Candida was still weepy, still droopy. Nothing interested her or made her smile.

Encyclopedia was getting hungry. Remembering the watchgoose's fate, however, he said nothing.

Suddenly Candida dried her eyes. "I just realized that I haven't eaten all day, and I'm starving," she announced. "Let's go have a snack."

As they sat at the kitchen table, Encyclopedia mentioned that he and Sally had discovered that they loved to cook.

Candida brightened. "We ought to have an Italian dinner for Columbus Day," she said.

"Bravo!" cried Sally. "Let's have the dinner at my house."

"No, here," insisted Candida. "We could have it to celebrate Columbus Day, the holiday, and in memory of Christopher Columbus Day, my poor departed goose. My mother will help us make her world-famous spaghetti sauce. We'll have marvelous, fantastic, earthshaking Italian food."

That settled the matter nicely. Encyclopedia, Sally, and Candida each invited a friend to honor both Christopher Columbus Days. They cooked and ate an Italian dinner at Candida's house.

Here is their menu:

Spaghetti
Italian Cheese Salad
Garlic Bread

Lemon-Orange Italian Ice

SPAGHETTI

- 2 tablespoons butter
- 2 tablespoons salad oil (use olive oil, if you have any)
- 2 tablespoons finely chopped onion (or 1 tablespoon instant onion)
- 1 large can (about 28 ounces) crushed, chopped, or ground tomato
- 1 6-ounce can tomato paste
- ¼ cup water
- 2 teaspoons oregano
- ½ teaspoon salt
- ¼ teaspoon black pepper
- ¼ teaspoon sugar
- 1 1-pound box spaghetti

You will need:
  large saucepan
  large pot
  colander

1. Melt the butter with the oil over low heat in a large saucepan. The pan should be large enough to hold all ingredients. Add the onion and cook, stirring constantly, for 3 minutes.

2. Add all the other ingredients except the spaghetti. Cook, uncovered, over very low heat for 20 minutes, stirring now and then. You can make the sauce ahead and reheat it at mealtime.

3. About 20 minutes before you want to eat, start heating a big pot of water. Cook the spaghetti according to the directions on the box. You'd better have a grown-up help you with cooking and draining it. After the spaghetti is drained, combine it with the sauce and serve.

Makes 6 big helpings. Some people like to have grated parmesan cheese on the table to sprinkle on their spaghetti.

ITALIAN CHEESE SALAD

    1 head lettuce
    1 medium tomato
    2 scallions
    ¼ pound Gorgonzola or blue cheese
    3 tablespoons salad oil
    1 tablespoon vinegar
    ¼ teaspoon salt

You will need:
    salad spinner or paper towels
    salad bowl
    small mixing bowl

1. Rinse the lettuce leaves in water. Dry them with paper towels or in a salad spinner.

2. Break the lettuce into very small pieces. Cut the tomato into small pieces. Chop the scallions by cutting a little piece off each end, removing and throwing away any dead leaves, then thinly slicing the stems crosswise. Put all these vegetables into a salad bowl.

3. Grate or crumble the cheese right on top of the ingredients in the bowl. Cover the bowl with foil or plastic wrap, then place in the refrigerator.

4. At serving time, combine the oil, vinegar, and salt. Pour over the top of the salad. Mix everything together.

Serves 6. If you don't like Gorgonzola or blue cheese, you can leave it out and substitute a can of chick peas or kidney beans, drained. It will be a different Italian salad, and just as good.

GARLIC BREAD

1 large clove garlic (or ¼ teaspoon garlic powder)
2 tablespoons soft (room temperature) butter or margarine
2 tablespoons salad oil
1 large loaf Italian or French bread

You will need:
garlic press (optional)
saucepan
bowl

1. If you're using a clove of garlic, put the garlic through a garlic press. Discard the peel. Combine the pulp, or garlic powder, with the butter and oil. Mix thoroughly. Let it sit for at least half an hour.

2. Cut the loaf of bread in half lengthwise. Spread the garlic mixture over the cut sides of the bread. Put the pieces, cut side up, on a baking sheet.

3. Preheat broiler. Shortly before you're ready to serve, broil the bread about 3 inches from the heat for 2 or 3 minutes—just until the garlic mixture is bubbling and turning brown. Watch closely, because it burns quickly.

4. After you remove the baking pan from the oven (remember to use oven mitts or thick potholders), put the two halves of the bread back together, so it looks like a loaf again. Cut down through it, crosswise, every 1½ inches to make single serving-sized pieces.

If you really love garlic, you can use 2 cloves instead of 1. That's the way Josh Whipplewhite likes his garlic bread.

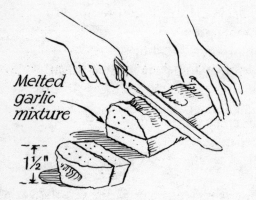

LEMON-ORANGE ITALIAN ICE

4 cups water
2 cups sugar
2 cups orange juice
Juice of 2 lemons

You will need:
medium-sized saucepan
10″ x 10″ baking pan

1. Combine the water and sugar in a medium-sized saucepan. Bring to a boil, stirring often, then boil over medium heat for 5 minutes.

2. Remove from heat until cool, then stir in the orange and lemon juices. Pour into a small (about 10″ x 10″) baking pan. Cover with foil or plastic wrap. Put in the freezer.

3. Let the mixture freeze undisturbed for half an hour, then stir it every half-hour for 1½ or 2 hours, until the ice is evenly frozen. Don't forget to do this, or you will have ice hard enough for the world's smallest skating rink instead of a good thing to eat.

CHAPTER 11
THE CASE OF THE SECRET RECIPE

BEAUFORD Twitty was eleven and crazy about potatoes. He was the only person in the United States who ran a potato museum. Admission was by invitation only.

"You're invited to the museum tomorrow at noon," he told Sally and Encyclopedia before the regular Friday afternoon touch football game. "I'm holding a potato tasting hour to introduce Tubers a la Twitty!"

"What's that?" Sally asked politely.

"Tubers a la Twitty is a secret recipe for preparing the world's newest potato," Beauford answered. "I can't tell you more now."

"How about one tiny clue?" Encyclopedia requested.

"Not about the recipe," Beauford said. "I don't want you to form an opinion before you taste it. But I can tell you about the potatoes that I'll use. They're superspuds."

He explained. His Grandfather Twitty, who had a farm in New York, had been trying for years to breed a better potato. He had finally succeeded.

"Those potatoes are the best," Beauford said. "Grandpa

sent me a bagful to test on the all-important kids' market. So I'm trying them out on you and some of my other friends. Tomorrow is D-Day."

"I'm sure Tubers a la Twitty will be delicious," Sally said breathlessly.

"It will be sensational!" Beauford proclaimed. "It will make the name of Twitty famous in the field. Look at Bismarck, Melba, Napoleon, Tetrazzini, Caruso, and Reuben. They gained undying fame. Why? Because recipes were named after them!"

Encyclopedia nodded knowingly. It was the best he could do when Beauford got carried away by his favorite subject, potatoes.

Beauford started for the door and stopped.

"I almost forgot," he said. "I have another surprise. My grandpa sent me a big potato with the autographs of all the Yankee pitchers. I'll display it at the tasting tomorrow."

With that he departed, walking lightly, as if he were stepping on potato chips.

A little before noon on Saturday, the detectives presented themselves at Beauford's front door. Already there were the other guests: Flo Landis, Darlene Cutler, Sean McCoy, and Farnsworth Grant.

At exactly twelve o'clock, Beauford opened the door.

"Come in and look around," he said. "I'll need another few minutes with Tubers a la Twitty."

The potato museum was in the basement. Strewn all about were potato bags, mashers, sacks, peelers, and even an old plow. There were also jars of Colorado beetles — the potato farmer's number-one enemy — and examples of some of the world's thousands of potato varieties.

"I've cleaned up the kitchen," Beauford called down. "We'll eat as soon as I set the table."

"Let us help you," Sally shouted.

The guests climbed the stairs and went into the kitchen. It was spotless. Everything had been put away.

"My folks let me use the kitchen provided it was clean when they returned from Glenn City this afternoon," Beauford said.

The guests did not stand around admiring the cleanliness. Each one found something to do. Darlene got the silverware. Sean and Farnsworth found glasses and filled them with water. Flo got out a bottle of ketchup. Sally fetched the paper napkins.

"You can take these," Beauford said to Encyclopedia, handing him a pair of candlesticks. "They'll add the proper touch of class."

When the table was set, Beauford put an old record on the phonograph. The scratchy sounds of Louis Armstrong tooting "Potato Head Blues" filled the dining room.

In the center of the table was a large bowl sealed across the top with aluminum foil. "Behold!" exclaimed Beauford. He whipped off the aluminum foil with a sweep of his arm. In the bowl were French fries.

Beauford grinned. "What did you expect, potato pancakes Rhineland style? Or *Pommes de Terre Farcies*? You shouldn't ruin magnificent potatoes with fancy cooking!"

The French fries were passed around. Farnsworth reached for the ketchup. Beauford howled in pain.

"You've got to taste them pure!" he cried.

The French fries were gobbled pure. They were the best French fries the guests had ever tasted.

"Think what a boon to the fast food industry my grandfather's potatoes will be," Beauford said, beaming with pleasure.

"What about the potato with the autographs of the New York Yankee pitchers?" asked Farnsworth, who at heart was a Chicago Cubs fan.

"Coming up," Beauford said. He hurried to the basement and brought back a small sack. Carefully he reached inside and pulled out a potato.

It was naked. There wasn't a single autograph on it.

Beauford sank weakly into his chair. "I've been robbed," he gasped.

"Who knew about the potato with the autographs?" Sally asked.

"Only you six," Beauford replied dully.

"Encyclopedia," Sally whispered. "Say something! Ask a question!"

Encyclopedia wondered if Sally thought he was a detective or a magician. Still, he did have one important clue. . . .

"Was the back door unlocked today?" he inquired.

"Y-yes," Beauford replied. "The doors are never locked during the day if someone is at home."

"Then excuse me," Encyclopedia said. He went outside and walked around the house. He stopped to peer into the kitchen.

When he returned to the dining room, he spoke to one of the guests.

"Would you kindly return the potato you stole?" he said softly.

WHO WAS THE THIEF?

(Turn to page 119 for the solution to
The Case of the Secret Recipe.)

CHAPTER 12

DINNER AT
THE TWITTYS'

ENCYCLOPEDIA had set right the world of Beauford Twitty. Flo had returned the potato with the autographs of the Yankee pitchers. The potato museum was back to normal — still a mess, but complete.

"I'm going to clean up the museum," Beauford vowed as he and Encyclopedia sat in the Brown Detective Agency on Sunday. "I have a great idea. The exhibits will be color-graded."

"How's that?" questioned Encyclopedia.

"My potatoes will be displayed by color, from skins of brownish white to deep purple," Beauford explained.

"Spruce up the spuds," Encyclopedia said, "and your museum could double as a modern art gallery. Imagine, art that can be eaten! You'll be the toast of two continents."

Beauford shrugged. "I'm not into modern art," he said. "I'm into potatoes. Anyone can understand potatoes. They don't need excuses."

Beauford got to his feet. "I stopped by to thank you for your detective work," he said. "And to invite you over for dinner tomorrow. I'm going to cook it all myself, without one potato recipe. Can you come?"

Encyclopedia accepted eagerly and added, "I'd like to help with the cooking."

"I can use help," confessed Beauford. "Come at five o'clock, then."

Encyclopedia arrived promptly at five. Here is the dinner he and Beauford cooked:

Cream of Chicken Soup

Meat Loaf
Corn Pudding
Baked Tomatoes
Lemon-Buttered Green Beans

Idaville Apple Pie

CREAM OF CHICKEN SOUP

Parsley, three or four sprigs, torn apart
2 10¾-ounce cans condensed chicken broth
1½ cups water
1 teaspoon salt
1 cup (1 8-ounce carton) medium or heavy cream
A dash of cinnamon

You will need:
scissors
saucepans (2)

1. Cut the parsley up with a pair of scissors. Don't use
the heavy stems, just the leaves and the tiny stems to
which they're attached.

2. Place the chicken broth, water, and salt in one saucepan, the cream in another. Warm both over low heat. Be
sure not to let the cream boil. Remove from heat.

3. Pour the cream slowly into the broth. Sprinkle on the
cinnamon. Stir. Sprinkle each serving with a little of the
parsley.

Makes 6 small servings or 3 or 4 bigger ones.

MRS. TWITTY'S MEAT LOAF

3 slices bread, crumbled
1 cup milk
1 egg

¼ cup minced onion (or 2 tablespoons
   instant onion mixed with 2 tablespoons
   water)
1 teaspoon salt
1 tablespoon Worcestershire sauce
1½ pounds ground beef
6 slices bacon (optional)

You will need:
   mixing bowl
   wooden spoon (optional)
   loaf pan

1. Preheat oven to 350°F.

2. Mix the bread, milk, egg, onion, salt, and Worcestershire sauce together in a bowl, then mix in the ground
beef. Use a wooden spoon or your hands.

3. If you're using the bacon, put 3 slices of it in a loaf
pan, lengthwise. Put the meat mixture in next, then top
with the other 3 bacon slices. If you're not using the bacon,
just put the meat loaf mixture in a loaf pan.

4. Bake for 1 hour and 15 minutes. Let cool for 15 minutes
after you remove it from the oven so it will be easier to
slice.

Serves 6. If there is any meat loaf left, you can have cold
meat loaf for dinner another night or make sandwiches
with the leftovers.

CORN PUDDING

    1 tablespoon soft butter or margarine
    2 eggs
    2 1-pound cans cream-style corn
    1 teaspoon salt

You will need:
    baking dish
    2 mixing bowls

1. Preheat oven to 350°F. (It will already be on if you're cooking this whole meal.) Grease a baking dish with the butter or margarine.

2. Beat the eggs a little with a fork in a small bowl or in a blender. Put the corn into a bowl and mix in the salt and the eggs. Put into the baking dish. Bake for 45 minutes. (If you're serving the whole dinner, put the corn pudding in the oven after the meat loaf has cooked for 45 minutes.)

Serves 6. To make half this recipe, use 1 can of corn, 1 egg, and ½ teaspoon of salt, but still use 1 tablespoon of butter to grease the baking dish.

BAKED TOMATOES

    3 medium-sized tomatoes
    ½ teaspoon salt
    1 tablespoon salad oil (plus a little more to
        oil the baking pan)
    4 tablespoons grated cheese

½ teaspoon dried oregano or basil

3 tablespoons soft bread crumbs (crumble 1 slice of bread with your hands)

3 tablespoons butter or margarine, cut into 6 slices

You will need:
small baking pan

1. Preheat oven to 350°F. (It will already be heated if you're cooking this whole meal.) Oil a small pan.

2. Wash the tomatoes in cold water. Cut them in half across the middle. Using your fingers or a small spoon, scoop out and throw away the seeds and the liquid around them. Sprinkle the tomatoes with salt, then turn them upside down on paper towels to drain for ten minutes. Now put them, cut side up, in the oiled baking pan.

3. Combine the salad oil, cheese, and oregano or basil. Stuff this mixture into the holes in the tomatoes where the seeds used to be. Sprinkle some of the bread crumbs on each tomato half, then press a slice of butter on top.

4. Shortly before you want to eat (after the meat loaf has cooked for 1 hour and 10 minutes), bake the tomatoes for 20 minutes.

Serves 3 or 6, depending on whether each person eats one tomato half or two.

LEMON-BUTTERED GREEN BEANS

2 packages frozen whole green beans (or 2 pounds fresh green beans)

4 tablespoons butter

½ teaspoon salt (plus more if you use fresh beans)

1 tablespoon lemon juice (the juice of ½ lemon)

You will need:

large pot

colander

large frying pan

1. Cook the frozen beans about 2 minutes less than the package instructions say. (If you use fresh beans, wash them, break off the ends, and cook them for 10 minutes in a big pot of boiling salted water — about 1 tablespoon of salt to 2 quarts of water.) Drain them in a colander.

2. Melt the butter in a big frying pan. Add the ½ teaspoon salt, then the beans. Cook over medium heat for 3 minutes, stirring carefully so you don't break the beans. Stir in the lemon juice.

Serves 6. To serve 3, use 1 package frozen green beans, 2 tablespoons butter, ¼ teaspoon salt, and 1½ teaspoons lemon juice.

IDAVILLE APPLE PIE

2 frozen pie crust shells

6 medium-sized apples (Red or Golden Delicious or Cortland are best)

⅓ cup granulated sugar
⅓ cup light brown sugar
¼ teaspoon cinnamon
⅛ teaspoon nutmeg
1   tablespoon cornstarch
2   tablespoons butter

You will need:
mixing bowl

1. Preheat oven to 450°F.

2. Thaw pie crust shells. Leave one in pie pan. Put the other on a flat surface for now. (It will be your top crust.)

3. Peel and core apples. Slice thin. Put slices into a bowl.

4. Combine both kinds of sugar with the cinnamon, nutmeg, and cornstarch. Sprinkle over the apple slices. Mix together gently. Put into crust in pie pan. Put little bits of the butter here and there all over.

5. Put the top crust on. Pinch its edge together with the edge of the bottom crust, then press flat against the top edge of the pie pan with the tines of a fork. Cut two or three slits in the top.

6. Bake at 450°F for 10 minutes, then reduce temperature setting to 350°F and bake for 35 minutes more.

Serves 4 to 8.

CHAPTER 13

THE CASE
OF
THE CHINESE
RESTAURANT

OLIVER Wilkie was fourteen and loved Chinese food. He was known by some as the Cantonese Kid. Others called him the Subgum Submarine because of the way he dived into any dish flavored with Oriental vegetables.

Whenever he had spare cash, he spent it at the Chinese restaurant near the junior high school. Usually he bought a takeout order of egg rolls or barbecued spareribs, which he ate by the duck pond behind the restaurant.

When he rang Encyclopedia Brown's doorbell, he looked as though a toothache would make him happy.

"I need your help," he said to the detective. "I could go to prison."

"Come in," said Encyclopedia. "You'd better sit down. What's the crime?"

"I'm supposed to have stolen a hundred and eight dollars," he said. "I didn't. The money disappeared from my schoolbag while I was in the Chinese restaurant Monday. The next day the restaurant went out of business."

"Oh," Sally said sympathetically.

"Oh, oh," corrected Oliver. "First I'm accused of stealing. Then the restaurant folds. I've been hit with a one-two punch to the head and stomach."

80

"Who says you stole the money?" Encyclopedia asked.

"Mitch Landon and Kate Walters," Oliver answered. "Since I beat Kate in the election for treasurer of the Service Club, she's had it in for me. She and Mitch are very close. They play mixed doubles on the tennis team."

"What do they say about the missing money?" Sally asked.

"I haven't time to tell you now," Oliver replied. "I'm already late for my piano lesson. But Monday at three o'clock there'll be a hearing in the principal's office. Can you be there?"

"Yes, and don't worry," Encyclopedia said. "Everything will turn out all right."

He spoke encouragingly, but he didn't feel encouraged at all. The case was like the start of an ice cream sundae. He didn't know what was going on.

Nonetheless, on Monday he and Sally joined Oliver, Kate, and Mitch in the office of Mr. Gerard, the junior high school principal.

As the detectives found seats, Mr. Gerard gazed at them questioningly. Oliver explained why they were there. Mr. Gerard nodded his permission for them to remain.

"This is not a trial," Mr. Gerard began. He was a soft-spoken man, popular with students and teachers alike. "We are here in an attempt to reach the truth about the missing money."

In a steady, quiet voice he reviewed for Encyclopedia and Sally the background of the case.

Each year, dues from all the school's clubs were put in the bank by the treasurer of one of the clubs. This

year the deposits were made by the treasurer of the Service Club—Oliver.

Before Oliver had set out for the bank, Mitch had handed him an envelope with money from the Lettermen's Club, of which Mitch was treasurer. Mr. Bertram, the club's advisor, had signed his name across the sealed flap of the envelope.

Oliver had put the envelope into his schoolbag along with those from the other clubs. On his way to the bank, he had stopped at the Chinese restaurant.

Because it was raining, he had decided not to go to the duck pond with a takeout order. Instead, he sat down at a table in the rear room.

A minute later, Mitch and Kate came in and took a table near his. It was after the lunch hour, and the three children were alone in the room.

Mr. Gerard looked at Oliver and then at Kate and Mitch. "Now," he said, "we come to the point of disagreement. I want your side first, Oliver."

Oliver cleared his throat nervously.

"After I'd sat down at the table, I noticed my hands were dirty," he said. "So I asked Mitch and Kate to watch my schoolbag while I washed. It was the only time I let my schoolbag out of my sight till I reached the bank and found the Lettermen's Club envelope missing."

Mr. Gerard thanked Oliver politely. Then the principal invited Kate and Mitch to tell their side.

"Oliver never spoke a word to us in the restaurant," Kate insisted. "When we got there, he was holding an envelope to the light. He slit it open with a table knife and peered inside. At that point he noticed us. He slipped the money from the envelope into his pocket, grabbed his schoolbag, and raced outside."

Mr. Gerard brought his fingers together and pressed the tips against his chin thoughtfully. "Does anyone have anything to add?" he inquired.

Encyclopedia raised his hand. "Sir," he said. "May I ask a question?"

"If you think it will help," Mr. Gerard answered.

"I'd like to ask Kate and Mitch if Oliver had placed his food order?"

"No," Mitch said. "Just as we sat down, a waiter brought a menu to his table. Find the waiter. He must have seen Oliver with the money in his hand."

"You can't find the waiter, and you know it!" Oliver cried. "The restaurant went out of business!"

"We do have one piece of evidence," Mr. Gerard said. He held up an envelope, slit open along the flap. "This is the envelope that held the Lettermen's Club money, according to Mr. Bertram, the club's advisor. He recognized it by his signature on the back."

Kate said, "When Oliver jumped up and ran out of the restaurant, he left the empty envelope behind."

Sally leaned toward Encyclopedia. "It looks very bad for Oliver," she whispered.

"Wrong," replied the detective. "It looks very bad for Kate and Mitch."

WHY?

(Turn to page 120 for the solution to
The Case of the Chinese Restaurant.)

CHAPTER 14

A CHINESE BANQUET

AMERICA's Sherlock Holmes in sneakers had done it again—cracked a seemingly uncrackable mystery.

Oliver was grateful but glum. "I'm giving up Chinese food," he said.

"Whatever for?" demanded Sally. "It's delicious."

"And dangerous," asserted Oliver. "Look where it got me. Into big trouble. I ask you seriously, who ever got ahead in life by eating Chinese food?"

"I Yin, for one," said Encyclopedia.

"Who's he?" Oliver asked suspiciously.

"He was a cook to King T'ang of Shang, founder of the T'ang dynasty in China," Encyclopedia said. "Eventually he became the king's prime minister. Some scholars say it was I Yin's skill as a cook that won him the job."

"From cook to prime minister?" Oliver gasped. "Really?"

"It's history," Encyclopedia said.

"You've made me feel better already," Oliver declared. "In fact, I'm getting hungry for some egg rolls and an order of sweet and sour meatballs."

"Oh, Oliver," Sally protested. "Have you forgotten? The Chinese restaurant went out of business."

"I did forget." Oliver moaned and bowed his head.

"Things aren't so bad," Encyclopedia said. "My mother cooks a Chinese dish now and then. We could take her recipes and put them all together. It would be a banquet!"

Oliver perked up. "Could I invite my little brother?"

"Bring him along," Encyclopedia invited. "We'll make enough for six."

And they did. Here's what they had:

Egg Drop Soup

Chinese Riblets
Egg Rolls with Chinese Sauces:
Duck Sauce
Hot Chinese Mustard Sauce
Sweet and Sour Meatballs
Chinese-style Rice

Oriental Fruit Cocktail

EGG DROP SOUP

6 cups chicken broth (you can make this with 3 10-ounce cans of concentrated chicken broth and 2¼ measuring cups of water)

2 eggs

1 big scallion (or 2 small ones)

2 tablespoons cornstarch combined with ¼ cup water

You will need:
    medium-sized saucepan
    small bowl or blender

1. Put the broth in a medium-sized saucepan. Start heating it over fairly low heat. Beat the eggs lightly in a small bowl or a blender. Trim a little off each end of the scallion. Slice it very thinly.

2. When the broth comes to a boil, stir in cornstarch mixture, then remove the pan from the heat. Pour in the beaten eggs with one hand while you stir the broth with the other, then stir in the slices of scallion.

Serve right away to 6 people.

CHINESE RIBLETS

½ cup soy sauce

½ cup honey

½ cup catsup

1 clove of garlic, crushed in a garlic press (can be left out if you don't like garlic)

½ teaspoon ground ginger

¼ cup water

3 pounds small pork spareribs or lean breast of lamb, cut in small sections of two or three ribs each

You will need:
    mixing bowl or pan
    baking pan

1. Combine the soy sauce, honey, catsup, garlic (if you're using it), ginger, and water. Put in a bowl or pan with the ribs. Make sure the ribs are well coated with the sauce.

2. Cover the pan with foil or plastic wrap, then place it in the refrigerator for about 3 hours. (If you don't have 3 hours to spare, you can skip this step, but it helps the flavor of the sauce to get all through the meat.)

3. Preheat oven to 325°F. Lift ribs out of sauce. Put them on a rack in a baking pan. Bake for 1½ hours, spooning some of the sauce over the ribs three or four times, until all of the marinade is used.

Serves 6.

EGG ROLLS WITH CHINESE SAUCES

Egg rolls are very hard to make from scratch, so buy the frozen ones. Follow the instructions on the package and allow one or two egg rolls for each person at the banquet. Serve the egg rolls with hot Chinese mustard and duck sauce (sometimes called plum sauce). You can buy these in most supermarkets, but it's more fun to make them.

DUCK SAUCE

½ cup plum jam or preserves
2 tablespoons apple sauce
5 tablespoons cider vinegar
1 teaspoon sugar

You will need:
small bowl

1. Stir everything together in a small bowl.

2. That's all!

HOT CHINESE MUSTARD SAUCE

2 tablespoons dry mustard
2 tablespoons water

You will need: small bowl

1. About half an hour before you want to eat, stir the mustard and water together. Place on a small plate or saucer.

2. Don't use more than a tiny bit of this—it's HOT.

SWEET AND SOUR MEATBALLS

For the meatballs:
  1½ pounds ground beef
  2 tablespoons finely chopped onion (or 1 tablespoon
     instant onion plus 1 tablespoon water)
  ½ teaspoon salt
  2 tablespoons salad oil

For the sauce:
  3 carrots
  2 green peppers
  2 tomatoes
  1 20-ounce can pineapple chunks, drained
     (save the juice)
  2 tablespoons brown sugar
  ¼ cup vinegar
  1 teaspoon salt
  2 tablespoons cornstarch
  ½ cup water

You will need:
  mixing bowl
  frying pan
  vegetable peeler
  medium-sized saucepan with lid

1. *Make the meatballs.* Mix the beef with the onion and
½ teaspoon salt in a bowl. Make it into balls a little
smaller than walnuts. Cook them in the oil in a frying
pan over moderate heat until they're brown—keep turning them over with a spoon as they cook. Remove pan
from heat.

2. *Prepare the vegetables. Carrots:* Peel (away from you) with a vegetable peeler. Slice as thin as you can. *Green Peppers:* Cut in two from top to bottom. Throw away the seeds and stem end; cut the rest into small slivers. *Tomatoes:* Cut in half; throw away the seeds and stem ends; cut into medium-sized chunks.

3. *Make the sauce.* Measure the juice you drained off the pineapple. Add enough water to make 1 cup. Put in a medium-sized saucepan with the brown sugar, vinegar, and 1 teaspoon salt. Bring to a boil; turn down heat. Add the carrots. Cover pan; cook for 10 minutes over low heat. Add the meatballs, green peppers, tomatoes, and pineapple. Then mix the 2 tablespoons of cornstarch with the ½ cup of water and stir this into the mixture in the pan. Keep on stirring, still over low heat, until the mixture comes to a boil and changes from cloudy-looking to clear. Remove pan from heat. Serve now, or reheat and serve later.

Serves 6.

CHINESE-STYLE RICE

You will need:
> strainer
> medium-sized saucepan with lid

1. Take 1 cup of long grain rice. Put it in a strainer. Hold the strainer under cold running water for 3 minutes, moving it around so all the rice is thoroughly washed.

2. Put the rice in a medium-sized saucepan that has a tight-fitting lid. Add enough cold water to cover the rice by 1 inch. Don't put the cover on the pan yet.

3. Bring the water to a boil over high heat, then let it boil hard for 4 minutes, or until most of the water has boiled off.

4. Turn heat very low. Put the cover on the pot. Cook for 15 minutes more. Stir with a fork before serving. Makes 3 cups rice, which will make a small serving each for 6 people. If you want more, just use more rice. The recipe always works, as long as you add water to cover the raw rice by 1 inch.

ORIENTAL FRUIT COCKTAIL

> 6 apples
> 1 8-ounce can water chestnuts
> 1 6-ounce can frozen orange juice, thawed
>   but not diluted
> 1 1-pound can crushed pineapple
> ¼ cup ginger marmalade

You will need:
     vegetable peeler
     mixing bowl

1. Peel and core the apples. Chop them into small pieces. Drain the liquid off the water chestnuts. Cut or slice them into fairly small pieces.

2. Put the chopped apples and water chestnuts into a bowl. Add the orange juice, pineapple, and ginger marmalade. Stir well. Chill until you're ready to serve.

Serves 6. If you can't find ginger marmalade in a grocery store, you can use ½ teaspoon ground ginger instead, plus ¼ cup orange marmalade. You can find water chestnuts in the Chinese section of most supermarkets.

This is a small Chinese banquet.

A large one might contain
chicken cooked three different ways,
lobster cooked two ways,
shrimp,
roast suckling pig,
a sweet and sour dish,
duckling,
beef cooked two different ways,
two or three fish dishes,
and three soups,
one of which is sweet
and is considered dessert.

CHAPTER 15

SNACKS
AND
LUNCHES

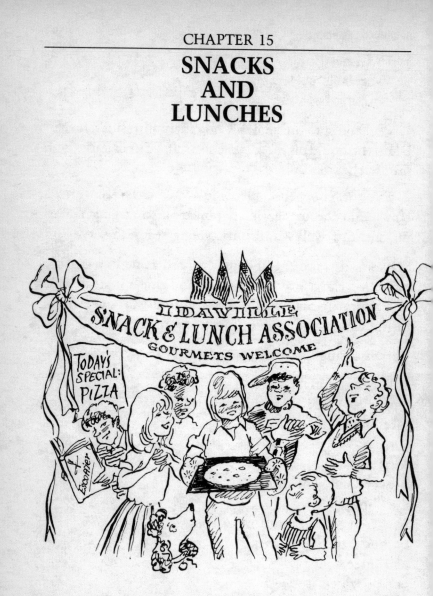

ENCYCLOPEDIA and his friends don't just cook dinners. Lots of times they fix snacks and lunches. Here are some of the things they make.

PIZZA

___

    4 loaves pocket bread (also called pita bread, Syrian bread, etc.)

    1 8-ounce can or small jar pizza sauce (or use some of the spaghetti sauce from page 61)

    8 tablespoons shredded mozzarella cheese

    4 tablespoons grated Parmesan cheese

    2 teaspoons oregano (or basil or Italian seasoning)

You will need:
  baking sheet

1. Preheat oven to 350°F.

2. Put the whole loaves of pocket bread, wrong side up, on a baking sheet. Spread about ¼ cup pizza sauce on each one. Cover all the bread except for a narrow border around the rim. Sprinkle part of the mozzarella cheese on each piece of bread, then do the same with the Parmesan cheese and oregano.

3. Bake for just 4 or 5 minutes, or until the mozzarella cheese is melted.

Makes 4 small individual pizzas. If you don't have mozzarella cheese, you can use cheddar instead. Also, if you can't find pocket bread in a store, you can use small loaves of French bread. (Cut them in two lengthwise first.) Split English muffins make good pizzas, too.

SLIPPERY JOES

1 teaspoon salad oil
1 pound chopped beef
¼ cup minced onion (or 2 tablespoons instant onion plus 2 tablespoons water)
1 cup catsup
4 hamburger rolls

You will need:
medium-sized frying pan or saucepan

1. Put the salad oil in a medium-sized frying pan or saucepan. Add the beef and onion. Cook and stir over medium heat until the color of all the meat changes from pink to light tan.

2. Stir in the catsup. Cook over very low heat, stirring often, for 5 minutes.

3. Split the hamburger rolls open. Spoon the Slippery Joe mixture onto the bottom halves, then cover with the top halves. Or, to make open-faced sandwiches, put the bun halves, cut side up, on plates, then spoon on the Slippery Joe mixture.

Makes 4.

HIDDEN VALLEY SANDWICHES

1 tablespoon butter or margarine
2 slices bread (whole wheat is good for this)
½ small apple, peeled, cored, and thinly sliced (eat the other half of the apple)

    1 tablespoon raisins
    2 slices cheddar cheese (use natural cheddar,
       if possible)

You will need:
    baking pan
    spatula or pancake turner

1. Preheat oven to 375°F.

2. Use the butter to grease a baking pan. Put the bread on this. On top of the bread, put a layer of apple slices, then the raisins, then the cheese.

3. Bake for 10 minutes or until the cheese is bubbly. Remove from the pan carefully with a wide spatula or pancake turner.

Serves 1 or 2. For plain open-faced grilled cheese sandwiches, leave out the raisins and apple. In this case, you may want to spread the top side of the bread with a little mustard before you put the cheese on it.

ALPINE SANDWICHES

    1 French roll or 2 slices bread (if you use
       bread, you'll also need 1 tablespoon butter
       or margarine)
    2 slices Swiss cheese
    2 very thin slices onion (optional)

You will need:
    baking sheet
    spatula or pancake turner

1. Preheat oven to 375°F.

2. Cut the French roll in half lengthwise. Put the pieces, cut side up, on a baking sheet. If you're using sliced bread instead, grease a baking sheet with 1 tablespoon of butter, then put the bread slices on that.

3. Cut the cheese into little pieces. Put them on the roll or bread. Top with the onion slices, if you're using them.

4. Bake for 10 minutes or until the cheese is bubbly. Remove from the pan carefully with a wide spatula or pancake turner.

Serves 1 or 2. Sometimes Encyclopedia likes to spread a spoonful or two of Italian salad dressing on the cut sides of the roll before he puts on the cheese and onion.

VOLCANO SANDWICHES

    2 tablespoons butter
    2 slices bread
    2 slices pineapple
    2 slices any kind of cheese
    1 banana
    1 tablespoon coconut

You will need:
    baking pan
    medium-sized frying pan
    spatula or pancake turner

1. Preheat oven to 375°F. Use 1 tablespoon of the butter to grease a baking pan. Put the bread on this.

2. Put a slice of pineapple on top of each piece of bread, then a slice of cheese.

3. Peel the banana, cut it in half across the middle, then cut each piece in half lengthwise. Melt the other 1 tablespoon butter in a medium-sized frying pan over medium heat. Cook the banana pieces in this, turning them carefully with two spoons, until they just begin to brown. Now carefully, still using a spoon in each hand, lift the banana pieces out of the frying pan and arrange them on the sandwiches so they will look like lava coming down. Sprinkle on the coconut.

4. Bake for 10 minutes. (Take a look at the sandwiches after 7 minutes, though, because you don't want them to burn.) Remove from the pan very carefully with a wide spatula or pancake turner.

Makes 2 sandwiches.

SPECIAL COLD SANDWICHES

You make most of these just the way you do a peanut butter and jelly sandwich. (Spread the filling on two slices of bread, put the slices together with the filling in the middle, cut the sandwich in two if you want to—and away you go.)

1. Use cream cheese on raisin or nut bread. This sandwich doesn't need anything else, but you can add raisins if you want.

2. Mash cream cheese with a few slices of ripe banana. (Eat the rest of the banana.)

3. Use peanut butter with sliced banana.

4. Use lettuce leaves instead of bread. Spread their inside part with mayonnaise. Fill with slices of bologna, ham, or cheese.

5. Spread slices of bologna, ham, or salami with cream cheese or any cheese spread. Either put two pieces together or roll each piece up. In either case, have the filling in the middle.

6. Spread pickle relish on one piece of bread. Top with a slice of cold, leftover meat loaf, then another slice of bread. Or don't use bread at all—just two slices of cold meat loaf, with pickle relish in the middle.

7. Use thin slices of peeled cucumber between pieces of bread that have been spread on the inside with mayonnaise.

8. Make a pickle sandwich: Use bread and butter pickles between slices of buttered bread.

9. Use cottage cheese and peach jam (especially good on whole wheat toast).

10. Use liverwurst and lettuce between slices of rye bread that have been spread on the inside with mustard and mayonnaise.

TUBERS A LA TWITTY

(Oven-Baked French Fries)

1 large potato per person, scrubbed but not peeled
1 tablespoon salad oil per potato
1 tablespoon water per potato
Salt

You will need:
   large bowl
   cutting board
   baking tins
   spatula or 2 big spoons

1. Preheat oven to 375°F.

2. Combine the oil and water in a large bowl.

3. Cut a sliver off one side of each of the potatoes so they will stay flat on a cutting board, then cut them into ⅜″ slices. Stack several of the slices together and cut down through them at ⅜″ intervals. Put the pieces into the oil and water and toss around until they're well coated. Repeat until all the potatoes are cut and coated.

4. Spread the potatoes out on one or more baking tins so that they are one layer deep and not touching each other.

5. Bake for 40 minutes, turning the fries over once with a spatula or two big spoons after they've cooked 20 minutes. Sprinkle with salt to taste.

FRENCH FRENCH TOAST

To make the toast:
>   2 eggs
>   ½ cup milk
>   Butter for frying
>   8 to 10 1½-inch slices French (or Italian) bread

To serve it:
>   Confectioners' sugar and jelly or jam
>   *or* Butter or margarine and syrup

You will need:
>   mixing bowl or blender
>   griddle or frying pan
>   pie pan

1. Beat the eggs and milk together in a bowl, just until they're blended. (If you have a blender, use it for this.) Pour into a pie pan.

2. Heat a griddle or frying pan over medium heat. Melt about a teaspoon of butter in it.

3. Dip both sides of the slices of bread into the egg and milk mixture. Fry on both sides until speckled brown. After each batch of bread is cooked, add more butter to the griddle or frying pan.

4. To serve, either sprinkle with confectioners' sugar and put a spoonful of jelly or jam on each slice, or serve with butter and syrup, just the way you would pancakes.

Serves 4 or 5. You can make regular French toast the same way by using slices of whatever bread you have on hand.

TANGERINOS OR TANGELINOS

    4 tangerines or tangelos
    ⅓ cup honey
    ½ cup chopped nuts, or ½ cup coconut

You will need:
    small mixing bowls (2)
    baking pans or pie tins

1. Separate the tangerines or tangelos into sections. Pull off any loose white strings.

2. Put the honey and the nuts or coconut into separate small bowls.

3. One at a time, dip the sections in the honey, then into the nuts or coconut. (Use your fingers to do this.) Put the fruit sections on baking pans or pie tins that will fit in your freezer. Make sure the sections don't touch each other.

4. Freeze for at least 1 hour. Eat while they're still frozen. Recipe makes a lot — how much depends on how many sections there are in each tangerine or tangelo.

If you use tangerines, call these Tangerinos.
If you use tangelos, then they're Tangelinos.

BANANA SMASH

    6 ripe bananas
    1 tablespoon honey
    1 tablespoon lemon juice (the juice of ½ lemon)

You will need:
  mixing bowl
  freezer container or small tin with lid

1. Put the bananas, honey, and lemon juice in a bowl. Mash it all together with a fork. (It doesn't have to be absolutely smooth, just well smashed.)

2. Put the mixture into a freezer container or small tin. Cover it and put it in the freezer for at least 4 hours (or for as long as 2 weeks). If the banana smash is very hard when you take it out of the freezer, let it sit at room temperature for about 45 minutes before serving. Good by itself or with cake or whipped cream/

Makes 4 big servings.

OATMEAL COOKIES

  ½ cup (1 stick) butter or margarine, at room
      temperature
  ½ cup light brown sugar (pack it down firmly
      while measuring)
  ½ cup white sugar
  1 teaspoon vanilla
  1 egg, unbeaten
  ⅔ cup unsifted flour
  ½ teaspoon baking soda
  ½ teaspoon salt
  1 teaspoon cinnamon
  1½ cups oatmeal (uncooked)

For all cookie recipes, you will need:
    baking tins (2 or 3)
    mixing bowls (2)
    spoon or electric mixer
    spatula or pancake turner

1. Preheat oven to 375°F. Lightly grease two or three baking tins (see below).

2. Combine the butter with both kinds of sugar and the vanilla and egg in a mixing bowl. Mix well with a spoon or electric mixer.

3. Mix the flour, baking soda, salt, and cinnamon together in a small bowl. Add this, bit by bit, to the butter mixture. Stir in the oatmeal.

4. Drop onto the baking tins by scooping up a slightly heaping spoonful of the cookie dough with a regular tea or coffee spoon, then pushing the dough off onto the tins with the back of the bowl of another spoon. Keep the cookies about 1½" apart, as they will spread. You can fit 20 to 24 cookies on a big tin. If your tins are small, you may have to use three of them or use the same one two or three times, regreasing it every time.

5. Bake, one tin at a time, on the top shelf of the oven for 8 to 12 minutes, or until the cookies begin to brown. Let them cool slightly on the tins, out of the oven, before lifting them off with a spatula. Makes about 40 cookies.

CHOCOLATE CHIP COOKIES

Follow the recipe for oatmeal cookies, but make these changes: Increase the flour to 1 cup; don't use the cinnamon; instead of using oatmeal, stir in 1 6-ounce package of semisweet real chocolate bits. (You can also add ½ cup chopped pecans or walnuts, if you like.)

COCONUT-OATMEAL COOKIES

Follow the recipe for oatmeal cookies, but add ⅓ cup coconut when you stir in the oatmeal.

RAISIN-OATMEAL COOKIES

Follow the recipe for oatmeal cookies, but add ¾ cup raisins when you stir in the oatmeal.

MONSTER COOKIES

Any of these cookies can be made in "monster" size. Use an ice cream scoop to measure and move the dough, then slightly flatten each mound with the back of a spoon. Bake only three cookies at a time.

ENCYCLOPEDIA BROWNIES

½ stick (2 ounces) plus 1 tablespoon butter
 or margarine
1 cup brown sugar, firmly packed in cup while
 measuring
1 egg

½ cup flour
⅛ teaspoon salt
½ teaspoon pure vanilla
1 6-ounce package semisweet chocolate bits

You will need:
8" x 8" baking pan
large saucepan
spatula or pancake turner

1. Preheat oven to 325°F. Use the 1 tablespoon of butter or margarine to grease an 8" x 8" baking pan.

2. Melt the rest of the butter or margarine over low heat in a saucepan large enough to hold all the ingredients. Remove from heat. Mix the brown sugar in well, then let cool for 10 minutes, or until lukewarm.

3. Stir the egg, then the flour, salt, and vanilla into the brown sugar mixture. Spread out evenly in the prepared pan. Sprinkle the chocolate evenly on top of the batter.

4. Bake for 25 to 35 minutes, or until the edges of the brownie mixture are pulling away from the pan and the top is shiny and somewhat wrinkled around the chocolate bits. (The mixture will still be very soft.) Let cool for 15 minutes, then cut into small squares, but don't remove from the pan until completely cool. Use a spatula to remove them.

These brownies are thin and chewy and seem almost like candy. If you'd rather have brownies with no chocolate at all in them you can substitute butterscotch or caramel bits for the chocolate ones.

SALLY'S DOUBLE-CHOCOLATE BROWNIES

½ pound (2 sticks) plus 1 tablespoon butter or margarine

4 ounces unsweetened baking chocolate

4 eggs

2 cups sugar

1 teaspoon pure vanilla

1 cup plus 2 tablespoons pre-sifted flour

1 6-ounce package semisweet real chocolate bits

½ cup chopped walnuts or pecans (optional)

You will need:

12" x 8" or 11" x 9" baking pan

double boiler

mixing bowl

electric mixer

spatula

1. Preheat oven to 350°F. Grease a 12" x 8" or 11" x 9" pan with the 1 tablespoon of butter or margarine. Put the 2 tablespoons of flour in the pan and tip it around until it covers the bottom of the pan. Shake any excess out into the kitchen sink.

2. Melt the rest of the butter or margarine and the unsweetened chocolate in a double boiler. Remove from heat; let cool for 10 minutes.

3. When the chocolate mixture is lukewarm, beat the eggs and sugar together in a bowl, perferably using an electric mixer, until they're thick and fluffy. With the

machine running slowly, add the chocolate mixture and the vanilla. Then, ¼ cup at a time, mix in the flour. Next, stir in the chocolate bits and the nuts (if you're using them) by hand.

4. Spread the batter evenly in the baking pan. Bake for 30 to 45 minutes, or until the top is shiny and the edges are pulling away from the pan. (The mixture will still be quite soft.) Cut the brownies into squares while they are still slightly warm, but don't remove from the pan until they are completely cool.

FROSTED CHOCOLATE

1 cup milk
¼ cup canned or bottled chocolate syrup
2 scoops vanilla ice cream

You will need:
blender or screw-top jar

Put all the ingredients into the container of a blender. Put the cover of the blender on tightly. Run the machine until everything is well mixed. (If you don't have a blender, put everything in a big screw-top jar with the top on tightly and shake, shake, shake it.)

Serves 1.

TROPICAL COOLER

1 cup unsweetened pineapple juice

10 medium-sized strawberries, either frozen (without sugar) or fresh

1 small scoop lemon sherbet, or Lemon-Orange Italian Ice from page 65, or Banana Smash from page 103

You will need:
blender

1. Put all the ingredients into the container of a blender. Put the cover of the blender on tightly.

2. Run the machine until everything is well mixed and slushy.

Makes 1 big drink.

CHAPTER 16

POINTERS
FROM
PABLO

THE two detectives were throwing a football in front of Encyclopedia's house when Pablo Pizarro, Idaville's greatest boy artist, stopped to watch.

"No cook should ignore the appearance of food," Pablo said out of nowhere.

Sally's eyes widened at the sight of him, and she fumbled an easy catch. "Hi," she breathed.

Encyclopedia never liked the way Sally mooned over Pablo. So he went directly to the point. "You've heard."

"Heard what?" Pablo asked innocently.

"Sally told the gang during the touch football game Friday that we were going to bake chocolate chip cookies today."

"Why, yes," Pablo admitted carelessly. "But I'd forgotten. I came by merely to help you and Sally."

"How thoughtful of you!" cried Sally. "I'm sure you can give us a real artist's view of cooking!"

"Naturally," Pablo said. "Artists have always been interested in the color, texture, and shape of food. Take van Gogh and Cézanne, to name only two. They were inspired by simple fruits and vegetables. They painted potatoes, carrots, apples, and watermelons."

Sally clapped her hands in delight. "Oh, Pablo, you know so much. You're full of things that aren't even in cookbooks!"

"Like sweet talk," Encyclopedia thought in disgust.

"The look of food is terribly important," Pablo went on. He was gazing softly at Sally, and he spoke as if Encyclopedia weren't there. "You must never forget how food is presented—how it is served has as much to do with cooking as does eating."

"I never thought of that," exclaimed Sally. "I want to hear more. Would you like some chocolate chip cookies? We took them out of the oven only half an hour ago."

Pablo shrugged. "If you insist."

As Sally led him into the house, Pablo mouthed on. "Serve hot food on hot dishes," he said, "and cold food on chilled dishes."

Encyclopedia managed not to kick him in the seat of his pants.

Sally lifted the cookies from the baking tin. She apologized for how they were served—on a paper plate covered with wax paper.

Pablo's smile was forgiving. "Sometimes the server is more important than the manner of serving," he said.

Sally blushed. Encyclopedia ground his teeth.

"I'll try just one," Pablo said.

Encyclopedia watched him eat seven in three minutes.

Before Pablo could reach for the eighth, Encyclopedia

was steering him toward the front door. On the way out, Pablo recited: "We may live without friends. We may live without books. But civilized man cannot live without cooks."

Encyclopedia closed the door after him, hard.

Sally frowned her disapproval. "You were downright rude. You all but threw him out."

"He got to me," Encyclopedia replied. "Why couldn't he come out and say he wanted some cookies instead of pitching all that arty stuff at us?"

"Oh, it's no use arguing," Sally said. "Let's forget it. Cooking is too much fun to be spoiled by anything so silly."

Encyclopedia agreed. "We can always bake more cookies," he said. "Maybe next time we'll *invite* Pablo."

Then he smiled at his thought. The Brown Detective Agency was closed for the winter, but the Brown kitchen was open all year round.

THE Tigers knew that if you eat parsley, it will take away bad breath, even the smell of garlic.

But they forgot they had eaten with their hands.

Unfortunately for them, Encyclopedia was on the case. He told Sally to sniff the hands of each Tiger.

"Garlic," she said over and over as she went from Bugs to Duke to Spike to Rocky. "Yuk!"

"You Tigers nearly got away with it," said Encyclopedia. "If you had washed your hands with strong soap, the garlic smell would have disappeared."

Sally laughed. "The Tigers wash their hands? Never!"

Trapped by their own mistake, the Tigers all chipped in enough money to pay Josh back for the ingredients for chocolate cake and garlic bread.

THE CASE OF THE FOURTH OF JULY ARTIST

THE Liberty Bell didn't crack until 1835. That was long after Nathaniel Tarbox Wiggins died. If he had seen the bell on July 4, 1776, or any other day of his life, he would have seen the bell without a crack.

When Encyclopedia pointed out this fact, the crowd of children lost interest in the raffle.

As Wilford was sadly folding his stepladder, Sally approached him. "That picture isn't half bad," she said. "Did you paint it yourself?"

"All by myself," Wilford replied. "It took me weeks to paint it and to rub it with dirt and give it lots of coats of dark shellac to make it look old."

The crowd of children and the parade were finished for the day. So was Wilford.

AT the party, Encyclopedia had asked Hermes, "Did you get your mother's gift?"

Since it was Hermes's birthday, anyone hearing the question should have thought Encyclopedia meant: Did you get the gift from your mother?

But Nancy Frumm said, "Yes, what did you get her?" That is, *for her.*

So Nancy knew Hermes had bought his mother a gift, and not the other way around. She could only have known this by overhearing Hermes talking with Bella and the detectives *while she was in the storeroom.*

Her slip of the tongue did not slip past Encyclopedia.

Nancy confessed. She had been biking down the alley when she saw the storeroom door ajar. She had sneaked in and stolen the two mixers.

IN Hector's Department Store, Encyclopedia had seen three piñatas fall off the counter. The clay jar broke. But the two papier-mâché bulls bounced. Had they been filled with candy, they would have been too heavy to bounce.

When Bugs claimed he had bought the piñata bull at Hector's, Encyclopedia got him to say he had just bought it "a few minutes ago." Therefore, it should still have been *empty!*

But Tim's aunt had stuffed it with a lot of candy. The number of stamps on the wrapping paper showed that the package had weighed more than a papier-mâché bull would weigh by itself.

Encyclopedia challenged Bugs to go to the store and weigh the piñata bull. Knowing it was full and heavy, Bugs refused.

But he gave Tim back the bull.

WHEN Candida's father learned from Encyclopedia who had stolen Christopher Columbus Day, he went directly to the state park.

The two men who had been roasting a "chicken" admitted stealing and eating the goose. Rather than have trouble with the police, they paid Candida's father far more than a goose is worth.

Encyclopedia nearly missed the clue—till Candida mentioned the tall woman's "dark brown shirt." The word "dark" triggered his memory. He realized the two men had lied. They'd been eating a goose, not a chicken.

A goose has only dark meat. The slice the men had cut off the breast and given Encyclopedia was *dark.* Had it really been from a chicken's breast, the meat would have been *white.*

FLO was the thief.

She had gone to Beauford's house twenty minutes early and looked into the kitchen window. When she saw that he was busy making French fries, she had sneaked into the museum by the back door.

After stealing the potato with the autographs and substituting an ordinary one, she had returned to the house shortly before noon for the tasting.

She confessed when Encyclopedia pointed out her mistake—the bottle of ketchup.

She would not have brought ketchup to the table unless she knew that Beauford's Tubers a la Twitty was not some fancy dish but simply French fries.

KATE wanted revenge on Oliver because he had beaten her in the election for treasurer of the Service Club.

So she got Mitch to help her steal the money belonging to the Lettermen's Club while Oliver was in the washroom. Then they blamed Oliver.

Encyclopedia saw through their story immediately. Oliver could not have opened the envelope "with a table knife."

In Chinese restaurants, knives are not part of the table setting. They are brought to the table only after the customer has ordered a steak or something that requires a knife to cut.

And Oliver had not yet ordered. As Mitch himself stated, the waiter was just bringing Oliver a menu when he and Kate sat down!

INDEX

Beans, Refried, 48
Beets, Pickled, 23
Brownies
  Encyclopedia, 106–107
  Sally's Double-Chocolate,
  108–109
Banana Smash, 103–104
Bread, Garlic, 63–64

Cake, Tooth Collector's
  Chocolate, 36–37
Chicken, Oven-Fried, 20
Chocolate, Frosted, 109
Chowder, Corny, 33
Cole Slaw, 35
Cookies
  Chocolate Chip, 106
  Coconut-Oatmeal, 106
  Mexican (Polvorones),
  51–52
  Monster, 106
  Oatmeal, 104–105
  Raisin-Oatmeal, 106
Corn Chips, 47
Cucumber Mouthfuls, 35

Egg Rolls, 89

French French Toast, 102
French Fries, Oven-Baked
  (Tubers à la Twitty), 101
Frosting, Tooth Collector's, 38
Fruit Cocktail, Oriental,
  92–93
Fruit Platter, 50–51

Garnishes, Mexican, 49–50
Green Beans, Lemon-Buttered,
  78

Italian Ice, Lemon-Orange, 65

Meatballs, Sweet and Sour,
  90–91

Meat Loaf, 74–75
Meat Mixture, Mexican, 49

Pie, Idaville Apple, 78–79
Pizza, 95
Polvorones (Mexican cookies),
  51–52

Pudding, Corn, 76
Riblets, Chinese, 88
Rice, Chinese-style, 92

Salad
  Italian Cheese, 62–63
  Potato, 22–23
  Tomato, 21
Sandwiches
  Alpine, 97–98
  Hidden Valley, 96–97
  Special Cold, 99–100
  Volcano, 98–99
Sauces
  Duck, 89
  Hot Chinese Mustard, 89
Shortcake, Red, White, and
  Blue, 24–25
Slippery Joes, 96
Soup
  Cream of Chicken, 74
  Egg Drop, 86–87
Spaghetti, 61–62
Stew, Toothburger, 34

Taco Shells, 47
Tangelinos, 103
Tangerinos, 103
Tostadas, 34
Tomatoes, Baked, 76–77
Tropical Cooler, 110
Tubers à la Twitty (Oven-
  Baked French Fries), 101

121

About the Authors

Donald J. Sobol has written many books in his quarter century as a writer. Perhaps the most popular of these are his Encyclopedia Brown books, of which this is the sixteenth. The fifteenth and fourteenth in the series, *Encyclopedia Brown Sets The Pace* and *Encyclopedia Brown Carries On* are also available as Apple Paperbacks, as is Mr. Sobol's first book about a girl detective, *Angie's First Case*. Mr. Sobol, originally from New York, now lives in Miami, Florida.

Glenn Andrews and her children have always been interested in the Encyclopedia Brown series, which motivated her to write recipes for *Encyclopedia Brown Takes The Cake!* Born in Chicago and raised in Connecticut, she currently resides in the Boston area. She has written several other cookbooks.